# The
# Tinker's Daughter

## A STORY BASED ON THE
## LIFE OF MARY BUNYAN

DAUGHTERS OF THE FAITH SERIES

# The Tinker's Daughter

## A STORY BASED ON THE LIFE OF MARY BUNYAN

### Wendy Lawton

**MOODY PRESS**
CHICAGO

*For Rebecca.*
*She loves her family*
*with a Mary Bunyan-like intensity.*

# Contents

1. Farewell at the Forge — 9
2. Black of Night — 21
3. Quarrel in the Kitchen — 29
4. Slough of Despond — 39
5. St. Andrew's Day Fair — 53
6. An Unusual Friendship — 63
7. Gypsies, Beggars, and Tinkers — 71
8. Putting the Pieces in Place — 85
9. Uproar at the Cottage — 95
10. Gifre's Attack — 105
11. The Healing Begins — 111
12. All Things Through Christ — 119
    Epilogue — 127
    Glossary — 129

# Farewell
## at the Forge

Clang, clink, clink. Clang, clink, clink. The sledgehammer beat a steady rhythm against the hot metal sheet on the anvil.

"Papa? What are you making?" Mary spoke loudly because of the roaring fire in the forge.

"When did you come in, wee Mary?"

"I have been sitting on the stool for a while, listening to you work." Mary asked her question again. "What are you making?"

"I am making a lantern," he answered, hitting the metal again.

Mary could tell by the sound that the metal was not yet thin enough for Papa to begin piercing the intricate patterns that would allow light to escape. Once the sheet had been perforated, he would shape the metal into a cylinder. How good it felt to sit beside the warm forge while her father worked the metal! The sounds and smells reminded her of the old times.

"I came out here to think," Papa said. "I can always think better with a hammer in hand."

"Do you want me to go back into the cottage so that you can be alone?"

"Nay, Mary." She heard him put his tools down. He closed the door to the forge. She could feel her father pull his bigger stool next to hers. "There. 'Tis much quieter. We haven't had a good talk in a long time." Her father's strong hands lifted her off her stool and into the familiar nest of his lap. She almost protested that she was *not* a babe in arms, but she wriggled deeper into the warmth and comfort instead. Inhaling the mixture of wood smoke, soap, and earth that mingled with the beloved scent of her father was a comfort not to be denied.

"'Tis a good thing you are still a wee mite, Mary."

"I am not . . ." Mary started to protest but she could feel the chuckles rumbling in her father's belly and she realized that he was teasing her. "Oh, Papa."

"You are no bigger than my anvil. But you are much more interesting."

"Will you tell me what you see . . . please?" Nobody could paint a picture with words the way her father, John Bunyan, could. Mary, blind since birth, lived for her father's descriptions. They made her feel as though she could see.

"Aye. Now then, where shall I begin? Picture a thick head of fine hair, curling slightly at the shoulder, eyes the color of this smooth piece of metal," he put a cold piece of metal in her hand, "and an uncommonly tickly mustache. I must confess —I am a handsome man. I stand taller than any in Bedford. I have—"

"Oh, Papa. Do not tease me so and stop tickling me with your mustache! I know what you are like. Everyone talks of you," she said, teasing him right back, "although never have I heard you referred to as handsome."

Papa's stomach bounced her as he laughed.

She felt shy asking, but the older she was, the more she wondered about herself. "Could you tell me what I look like?"

How Papa loved to tease his children. It was hard to get a solemn answer from him. "You may be a little bigger than my anvil." He lifted her high into the air, feet dangling. "Hmm, I would say about five *stone* in weight."

"I know the lightness of my frame, but I also know I am as strong as an ox." She was getting exasperated. *Don't fathers ever know when to be serious with their daughters?*

Her father settled her on his knees. "Well, little daughter, I must admit that you are passing fair."

"You mean I am pretty?"

"You have curls the color of wild honey warmed by the fireplace." He pulled on one of her ringlets.

Mary was forever trying to pull Mama's tortoise-shell comb through her tangle of curls, but she loved the picture of warm honey. The smooth richness of honey was hard to forget, even in this month of November. Each summer the honey was warmed so that the wax of the honeycomb would float to the surface. The smell was not easily forgotten. And the taste . . . "I do like the sound of that color." She waited for him to go on.

"Your eyes are the same gentle blue of your mama's silky ribbon." His voice had become as soft as the well-worn ribbon.

Mary slept with that ribbon each night since her mama died and kept it tucked in her apron pocket by day.

"Your mama was a beautiful woman, Mary," her father said, reading her thoughts. "She had the same honey hair as you, but instead of your curls, hers was smooth and straight." He sighed, and the slow intake and release of breath shifted Mary ever so slightly on his lap. "When we wed, she brought me the most valuable dowry a man could obtain."

*Dowry.* The word sounded familiar, but Mary could not place it. "What is a dowry?"

"When a couple marries, the girl's family shares its wealth with the newlyweds. Most often it is silver coins or even gold, but your mama's dowry was far more valuable." He paused and Mary waited for the story. "She brought two books with her to the marriage: *Plain Man's Pathway to Heaven* by Pastor Arthur Dent and *Practice of Piety* by Lewis Bayly."

Mary heard a scuffling sound by the far window and another sound that caused fear to grip her stomach—a cynical laugh that could only belong to Gifre. "Did you hear that, Papa?" asked Mary.

"Hear what?"

"I thought I heard Gifre sneaking around outside." Perhaps she was wrong.

"No, I heard nothing over the din of the forge, but my hearing is not as sensitive as yours. Has that boy been bullying you again?" Papa asked.

"He never stopped, but I do not allow it to worry me." Mary stiffened her back. After all, he would not risk hurting her . . . would he? "But we were speaking of Mama's dowry— you said the books were valuable. More valuable than gold?"

"These were," her father answered, "for they helped me find my way to the Truth." He paused. "Never have I hidden my own rough youth from you, Mary. It was said that there was no one in the village of Elstow who could blaspheme like the young tinker, John Bunyan. I am not proud of it, mind you, but it is a fact."

"And these books taught you how to stop cursing?" Mary asked.

"Oh, no, I could never have changed my life by myself. They pointed me to the One who would change me. Your mama helped set me on the path too. No question about that."

"If you tried hard enough, surely you could have conquered the habit," Mary said with determination.

"My fiercely independent little daughter," her father said, sighing. "You'll have your own arduous journey to make until you learn that you cannot do it in your own strength. I doubt not that you will come to Christ, but you shall have to discover the Truth on your own, just as I did."

"Tell me what you mean, Father."

"You have spent so many years proving that you are little hindered by blindness that you have developed a fearsome determination. Your toughest lesson may be learning how to depend on God and on other people." Papa was quiet for a time. "Your mama would be proud of you, Mary. Look at how much you have done since she has been gone. You are scarcely ten years old, yet you have helped your sister care for the household and you have been a little mama to Jake and Thomas."

"I loved doing it, Papa. Bets and I were a team until—" Mary realized she had said too much. Papa had married Elizabeth the year following Mama's death. Elizabeth was kind, with a soft voice and gentle hands. Bets said their new step-mother was pretty, but she was only seventeen years old. Seventeen. Just seven years older than Mary. There was no way Elizabeth could ever be a mama to Mary.

"Mary, you are the oldest child and I know you had a hard time accepting Elizabeth." After giving Mary a chance to reply, he continued. "I never thought I would be able to love again after your mama died, but Elizabeth was a gift from God. Coming into our family of four children cannot have been easy for her, but she has done her best to ease the burden."

"I know, Papa." Mary hung her head as Papa continued to talk.

"I had hoped you would be friends long before this, and now with the new baby on the way . . ." His arms enfolded her as he rocked her back and forth as if she were the baby. She wished she could stay like this forever, even if she was almost grown.

"I will try, Father. I will try much harder."

"You will, lass. I value your strength. If anything were to happen, you would be one to depend on."

Mary shivered. *If anything were to happen.*

Ever since he started preaching about four years ago, things had not been the same. How odd that her father was at the center of this whirlwind of English politics and religion. She remembered when he worked as a tinker in Elstow. How she yearned for the days when he spent his time mending pots and kettles and fashioning things out of metal.

The trouble had started several weeks earlier with warnings. Late at night men came to the cottage to speak with her father. "You must stop preaching," one warned. "Word is out that in spite of promising tolerance, the parish churches are pressuring King Charles to do something about the *nonconformists.*"

Another voice chimed in, "Ever since the *royalists* managed to get Charles on the throne they have been anxious for a restoration of their former power." The voice grew more insistent. "They see you as a threat."

"They do not endure threats lightly," the first voice warned.

Mary recalled the sound of Father shifting his stance. By the thud of his firmly planted feet, she knew that he was not going to budge.

"Thank you, brothers, for the warning," he had said. "I know that you did so at great risk to your own families. I wish it did not have to come to this, but we made too much progress to allow our freedoms to be swallowed by the state church's bid to regain power."

They argued for hours. Much of it was confusing to Mary, but she understood that her father was too visible and too successful as a lay preacher to go unnoticed. The people who assembled to hear him talk about the Lord had begun to number into the hundreds. Papa made words come alive. No one could make Mary see more clearly than Papa. He seemed to have that effect on everyone.

When they left, Mary had hundreds of questions for her father. "Why are we in trouble, Papa?"

"'Tis not 'we' who are in trouble, wee Mary, 'tis I."

"What did you do wrong?"

"God called me to preach and I answered that call. During Cromwell's time we worshipped with complete freedom outside of the state church. Were it just a few years earlier, my activities would be perfectly legal. Now—who knows?"

"Can you simply stop preaching?"

"No, lass. I spent many years of my life wandering from God. If I have learned but one lesson, it is that I would sooner face danger in partnership with Him than a life of ease apart from Him."

"What will happen if you continue?" Mary could not imagine life without Papa.

"I am afraid it will go hard on us, Mary. Unless something intervenes, I will be arrested. If I still don't agree to give up my calling, I will be sent away from England, or worse." He paused. "Are you sure you want to hear the answers to your questions?"

"Aye, Papa."

"Aye." Her father sighed. "Never have I seen a one like you, Mary. You are a child in years only—you have borne more than your share of burdens." She found herself in her favorite place, sitting on Papa's lap, surrounded by his great, gentle arms.

"How I pray that you learn you cannot carry your burden alone."

* * *

"Mary, what are you thinking about?"

They were still sitting by the forge, but Mary's mind had been miles away.

"I was thinking about the trouble. Do you think—" Mary heard the cottage door slam and Bets calling for Papa.

"In here." Papa put Mary down, but held on to her hand. She could hear him breathing slowly, as if to fortify himself.

"Papa! There are men coming," Bets announced breathlessly. "Elizabeth says it is the constables." Mary could hear the quiver of fear in Bets's voice. Bets was just ten months younger than Mary and they had been each other's confidants for as long as they could remember. It took a lot to scare Bets.

"Girls, into the cottage by the back door. I shall close the forge and follow."

Papa had barely gotten into the house when they heard a ferocious pounding on the front door. The battering continued until the door was opened and Papa was summoned. Mary crowded close to Papa so she could tell what was happening. The constable with the heaviest tread—the one who smelled of roast *mutton*—cleared his throat with an explosive harrumphing sound and then began reading in a self-important voice. She could only catch snatches of the unfamiliar words.

". . . an upholder and maintainer of unlawful assemblies and conventicles." He made more phlegm-clearing noises. She could hear a crowd gathering outside the open door. ". . . not conforming to the National Worship of the Church of England."

He was arresting Papa for unlicensed preaching. "John Bunyan, you are under arrest and sentenced to perpetual banishment by order of his majesty, Charles II, King of England." Perpetual banishment! Her stomach twisted. That meant that he was to be sent away from England forever.

Mary heard the crowd milling outside the open door.

Some were even weeping. As her father slowly gathered his things, she heard a thud and felt the shudder of something heavy hitting the floor. Someone outside shrieked, "Elizabeth has fainted."

Mary moved to where Elizabeth had been standing. Her father leaned close to her ear. His voice was broken—so different from the playful, teasing voice in the forge. "Mary, take care of Elizabeth. If you can, please get word to me at the Bedford *Gaol* that everything is well—or find someone to send a note to me—anything. Anything." He kneeled on the floor by his unconscious wife for what seemed to be the longest time. Was he praying? Was he crying? She heard him kiss Elizabeth.

Mary could hear her sister Bets bring the baby to their father. As usual, Bets was trying to be strong, but Mary could sense the wad of sorrow groaning in Bets's chest. Two lingering kisses and murmurings—one must have been for Bets, the other for little Thomas. She felt the whoosh of air as her brother rushed over and she heard the sound of her father ruffling seven-year-old Jake's hair.

At last he drew Mary tightly to his side. "Oh, wee Mary . . ." The rest of the words seemed lost in his throat. He ran his calloused fingers down Mary's face, as if to savor its softness. His kiss on her forehead was as gentle as the stroke of a feather. As he dipped his hand into her honey hair, she felt him let it curl around his finger. She reached her hands up to memorize his face and touched wetness on his cheeks.

He gently took her hands away. "Take care of them, Father God," he whispered.

His body seemed loath to move, but she could feel him

tighten with resolve as he stood. His reluctant steps vibrated on the bare floor as he moved toward the door, speaking to the crowd outside. "Leaving my family is like pulling the flesh from my bones." The words seemed to be ripped from his very soul.

# Black
## of Night

$\mathcal{M}$ary woke with a start. Something was wrong. She moved her hand along the floor to the mat against the wall and felt both sleeping children. She touched the blanketed mound to her left and was satisfied. Her two brothers and sister slept. A moment of stillness, then she heard the restless creak of bed ropes below her sleeping loft.

*Elizabeth. Something is wrong with Elizabeth.*

Mary eased off the *pallet,* careful not to disturb the other children. Slipping her arms into her thin robe, she slid her hand along the wall to the bannister and undertook the steep stairs. Feeling the edge of each well-worn plank with her bare toes, she reached with the opposite foot to the step below. She quickly repeated this familiar motion, counting one . . . two . . . three . . . all the way till she leapt over the sixteenth step to land on the rough wooden floor. She hurried to the tiny bedroom alcove just off the common room. Whether from being startled awake or from the awful fear that something else was going wrong, she couldn't tell, but her heart was thumping so hard she could feel the drumming in her ears.

"Elizabeth?" She moved in closer and could hear her stepmother's labored breathing.

"Mary, is that you?" Elizabeth's damp hands pulled her to the bedside. "Something is very wrong. 'Tis not time for the baby yet." The young girl could feel tremors of fear as the clammy hands began to tighten. Elizabeth, now writhing, whispered her name, clenching her teeth on the last desperate syllable. Mary heard each separate wave of pain in that prolonged "eeeeeee" of her name.

When the pain subsided, Elizabeth loosened the grip on Mary's hands. "You must get help. Do you know where Midwife Dunkirk lives?"

"Aye. I think so."

"Please bring her back here. Things are not as they should be." Elizabeth's breathing reminded Mary of the heaving of a blown horse, as if the very act of pulling air into lungs was painful. "Do you need Bets or Jake to go along?"

"No." Mary thought of her brother and sister sleeping upstairs. Seven-year-old Jake would love the adventure of going out into the night, but he could be such a pest. She hated to have to explain everything to him. And Bets—well, Bets already did more than her share of work. "I can go alone."

"Go then," she said, "and Godspeed."

Mary quickly moved around the obstacles in the dark room. She took off her robe, hung it on her peg, and pulled her dress on over the top of her *chemise*. She reached for a pair of warm woolen stockings that had been drying on the hearth and yanked them over her cold feet. Her shoes stood precisely where she had placed them at bedtime, making it easy to quickly slide her feet into them. Taking her cloak from the peg by the entry, she unlatched the door and moved into the chill November night, closing the door behind her.

The dampness hit with a jolt of reality. She shrank back against the cottage wall. *What am I doing out here? How am I to find the midwife? Oh, Papa! Can anything more go wrong?* Mary turned around and opened the cottage door to reclaim the safety of home.

"Mary, is that you?"

How could she let Elizabeth down? This was the first time that Elizabeth had needed Mary's help. Had she not promised Papa to try harder to accept Elizabeth? She was as frightened by the events of the last few days as Mary and the children were. And now this.

"Yes, Elizabeth. I forgot my cane." Mary was too embarrassed to admit that fear had driven her back into the cottage. "I shall be so much faster if I use it." She went to the recess under the stairs and retrieved an odd-looking cane. It was long and slender with an intricately worked metal tip. As she touched its familiar handle, she remembered the care with which Papa had crafted it.

"A cane, Mary," he had said, "will be a valuable tool. It will extend your touch and allow you to move with confidence. Listen to the sounds of the metal tip on the cobbles. Feel the vibrations of moving cartwheels through the wood. Hear the splash of a puddle against the shaft."

*Move with confidence. Yes, that is what I must try to do,* Mary thought. *Thank you, Papa.* She moved out into the cold once again, her cane moving with a delicate cadence across the cobblestones. The chunk of fear crowding her heart started to melt as she fell into the familiar rhythm of movement.

Tap, tap, thud, tap. Mary could judge the wall to her right. Tap, tap, thunk. The gutter. She remembered to step over the filth that ran in the open ditch and to cross the road. She knew she had a long way to go. At the next crossroad, she turned to her right as she hit the wobbly cobblestone. The smell of the gardenia creeping over the wall of Goodwife Harrow's wash yard was a welcome relief from the stench of the street.

*Move with confidence.* It reminded Mary of a favorite verse that Papa often repeated as he led her along. "I can do all things through Christ which strengtheneth me."

Her father had come to depend on God for everything. Mary did not mind because Papa was so very strong already, long before he became a Christian. It was different for Mary, though. She hated the idea of being dependent on anyone— even God. She wanted to learn to be strong all by herself. Much of the time she felt weak and frightened, though she always tried to hide it. *Oh, how I wish I were confident and strong like Papa,* Mary thought.

She repeated the first part of the verse over and over as she walked with measured rhythm. "I-can-do-all-things . . ." She did not realize that she always left the second part of the verse off. "I-can-do-all-things . . . I-can-do-all-things . . ." The familiar phrase seemed to strengthen her.

She felt the missing cobble and then the wooden fence. *Gifre's house.* She knew it was too early for him to be about, but her heart began to thud louder.

Ever since the Bunyans moved from Elstow to Bedford, Gifre had taken an unnatural delight in tormenting Mary, missing no opportunity to taunt her with her most hated words, "Poor blind Mary." When he said it, there was no pity in his voice—just ridicule.

Mary never understood why Gifre was so angry. She knew that his father had lost much during the years of the *Protectorate,* but all of that had been restored. He was a staunch opponent of Papa's, but many in Bedford differed politically and still remained polite. Perhaps she would never know the cause of the anger that ruled Gifre. What she did know was that she tried to stay as far away from the boy as possible. He frightened her, much as she hated to admit it.

Her cane did little good along this dirt stretch, but she knew by counting steps she must be nearing the lacemaker's cottage where she must turn left. Aye, the cobblestones began again.

She smelled the yeasty scent of the malt beer fermenting in kegs in the brewery alongside the Crown Pub as she turned onto High Road. It was a welcome sign, however smelly, that she was making progress. The wood smoke from the baker's oven mingled with the malty odors. He must be getting ready to put the raised loaves into the oven so that they would be ready to deliver at daybreak.

Just the thought of bread made her stomach rumble. She knew the baker started with *maslin,* the dry brickle bread that was the daily fare of the poorest citizens of Bedford. It did not matter if it was cold by morning, for it was no better warm than it was cold. Mary knew that the diminishing hoard of coins in the family coffer was all that stood between the Bunyans and *maslin*—or worse. *I must come up with some way to feed our family.* And it was more than food that they needed.

Jake's sole was nearly off his shoe. Every time Mary heard that peculiar slap of leather as he walked or ran, she considered it a warning. *How are we to eat, let alone buy new shoes? Save that worry for later,* she scolded herself. *Only one problem at a time.*

As she made her way toward the midwife's house she heard the gnawing, scratchy movement of rats scurrying nearby. The stench reminded her that the sewage gullies belonged to the rats. She was the intruder.

The thought made her shiver. Every time Jake tried to describe rats to her, he used words like evil, foul, stinky. Jake was good at word descriptions, but he was terrible at helping Mary conjure up pictures. When he tried to make a word picture of a rat, she kept getting it mixed up with her idea of puppies—furry, long tail, sharp teeth. Mary loved the feel of a puppy, especially when it lay sleeping with its rounded tummy full of milk or when it pushed its damp nose against her, trying to get her attention.

She must ask Papa for a word picture of rat. The jailer at Bedford *Gaol* had sent word that if the prisoners were to eat, the families must provide food. She soon would visit Papa.

*Oh, Papa, I miss you! How will we live without you? How could you leave us this way?* Her thoughts tumbled in the same fearful circles that had consumed her the last few days. *How will we . . . ? Why did they . . . ? Whatever will become of us?*

Mary shivered again and decided it was easier to think about rats than to think of her father in Bedford *Gaol. At least he is still in Bedford and not banished to faraway Barbados as many others have been.* She could not bear to think about life without Papa.

Something bumped against her cane. Perhaps she was just as happy that she could not bring to mind a precise picture for rat. The furtive movements on all sides made her shudder, so she decided to try to picture puppies instead of rats. It did not help overmuch. She knew she would faint if one of the rats pushed its nose against her. Better to not even think about it.

Tap, tap, tap. She continued to make her way through the streets of Bedford. "I-can-do-all-things . . . I-can-do-all-things . . ."

Tap, tap, clink, clink. *The metal fence. I've reached the corner of Castle Lane and High Road. At last—the Dunkirk house!* "Please, oh, please, let the midwife be home," Mary whispered to herself.

# Quarrel in the Kitchen

Mary tucked her cane under her arm and followed the iron fence up the walk to the doorstep. Her hands were so cold, she could barely make a sound as she knocked on the midwife's door. Using the metal tip of her cane as a knocker, she rapped as loudly as she could. While she waited, she could feel the warmth of her own breath against the frigid air as it escaped in rapid, quivery puffs. *Perhaps someone else engaged the midwife this night. What if no one answers my knock?* A knot began to form in her stomach. *Could I have arrived at the wrong house?*

With tears stinging the back of her eyelids and a lump of anguish welling up in her throat, she knocked frantically. *Will I be able to retrace my steps? Did I remember to turn right . . . or was it left?* Just when the thumping of her heart began to pound louder than her own knocking, she heard movement on the other side of the door.

Midwife Dunkirk yawned noisily as she opened the door.

"Am I needed?" she asked. The midwife stamped her slip-pered feet against the cold. "I cannot recall any who are at term."

Mary could hear the rubbing of rough hands over a dry face.

"Why, 'tis poor blind Mary Bunyan. However did ye get here?"

Mary grimaced. "I came to seek your help. I am thankful to find you at home." Relief flooded Mary. She could almost ignore the midwife's reference to "poor blind Mary." Luckily, the midwife would never know how profoundly Mary had felt a few seconds earlier. It was not a feeling she often experi-enced, nor was it one she cared to undergo again. "Elizabeth is unwell. Please hurry."

"Dunkirk, get the cart hitched. I must go see to young Elizabeth Bunyan." As if by magic, the midwife became all business. Mary was quickly ushered inside and urged to sit by the hearth. An embrace of warmth enveloped her. Opening and closing cupboards told her that the necessary supplies were being gathered as Midwife Dunkirk bustled about the room. The woman had a comforting habit of talking to her-self. "That poor little family . . . I don't know why troubles come in patches . . . ." The muttering grew less intelligible as she went about her tasks.

"May I help?" Mary thought it was taking a very long time.

"Oh, goodness no, child." The fumbling continued. *"Leeches,* cannot forget the *leeches."* Hinges creaked, then came the rattle of waxed paper being unfolded. The pungent aroma of herbs wafted through the room as she packed them. A pause. "Dunkirk?"

"Aye?"

"Is the cart hitched?" Mary could tell that the husband-and-wife team had worked together for many years. A complicated, familiar ritual of anticipating each need was played out between them.

"Aye. The cart is hitched and waiting outside the fence. We be all ready for ye." He had a lilt to his voice.

"And the blankets?" Continuing to mumble, the midwife never slowed her pace as she gathered the tools of her trade. Mary heard the heavy scrape of a glass stopper sliding out of the rough glass neck of a bottle. She identified the tinkle of *apothecary vials* pushed next to one another. "Where is that little *casket* of cobwebs? Those I use to stop bleeding?"

"Coo. I left it over to the shed. Replenishing your supply, I was." His voice rapidly moved away. "Let me fetch it and meet ye in the dooryard. Put the *firebell* over wots left o' the fire and tuck a flask o' *hippocras* in yer bag, will ye?"

"Lord love him, Mary. A finer man ye'll never find." A woolen blanket was wrapped 'round her shoulders. Drowsy with the warmth of the hearth and the soft murmurings and bustle of the midwife, it took Mary a moment to realize that it was time to leave.

"Are you ready, Midwife Dunkirk?" Mary asked.

"Almost. Let me lace myself into something decent and meet ye at the cart." She started to move away. "Do ye need help getting out to the dooryard, Mary?"

"No." Mary tucked her anger inside as she made her way outside. *How do you think I got here in the first place? Do I look* daft *as well as blind? Will no one ever realize that I am not only capable of caring for myself, but my papa charged me to care for our whole family?*

"Mary Bunyan, ye look to be miles away," the old man said, startling her out of her reverie. "Ye almost walked into Dobbin. He be a patient horse, but 'twould not be healthy to come at him from his backquarters."

"I am sorry, Neighbor Dunkirk. It has been a long night."

"Dinna ye worry, lass. She will be right out. She's a right one, that missus o' mine. She will take care o' yer Elizabeth. Never ye mind, now." His voice was soothing and his words measured, as if he were calming a skittish animal. He helped Mary up into the back of the cart and tucked warm robes around her. Soon the cart settled with the weight of the midwife, climbing up beside her husband.

*Must weigh at least thirteen* stone, Mary thought drowsily.

Clip, clop, clip, clop. The horse plodded through the quiet streets retracing Mary's earlier journey.

❧        ❧        ❧        ❧

"Why didn't you wake me?" Bets whispered through clenched teeth, emphasizing each word with a staccato burst of movement, pacing around the tiny lean-to kitchen. Mary felt the percussion of Bets's anger.

Midwife Dunkirk was in the alcove with Elizabeth. The boys still snored upstairs. From the stillness in the loft, Mary guessed that they were tightly intertwined in a tangle of covers on their *pallets,* oblivious to the emotional storm raging around them. How Mary wished she were upstairs, tucked in that warm cocoon with two-year-old Thomas and their brother Jake.

"I never even thought to wake you." Mary had a feeling that her sister was not even listening.

"I knew nothing. Nothing! How could you go off like that without waking me? I did not even know anything was amiss until I heard Elizabeth crying for Papa." Bets's voice shook with anger.

"I had it well in hand, Bets." Mary laid a hand on Bets's arm to calm her, but her sister jerked away. Mary continued in a soothing voice, "There was no reason to wake you or the children. I went to get the midwife. I brought her back, didn't I?"

"You had it in hand?" Bets was furious. "I forgot, Mary. You alone are completely sufficient." She bit off each word, her voice rising with each syllable. "I doubt not that you believed you could do it all. You do not need anyone . . . you do not need anything. . . you certainly do not need me!"

"Shhhhh. Please do not disturb Elizabeth." Mary had never heard her sister so angry.

Bets was only ten months younger than Mary and had always been calm and steadfast. Nothing ruffled her feathers. Nothing, that is, until now. When their mother died less than two years ago, Bets had pitched in and worked alongside Mary, cooking, cleaning, and caring for the boys. Bets was the one who had been closest to Mama, but she never let the grief overcome her. She used to tell Mary that she could only live morning by morning, trusting God to get her through that one day.

When Papa brought Elizabeth home and told them that

she was to be their new mama, it was Bets who welcomed her and helped the others make a place in their hearts for her. Mary was not so generous. Until that time, Bets had always gone by her given name of Elizabeth. When Papa remarried, she laughed about it and good-naturedly suggested they all adopt Mary's nickname for her to lessen the confusion. So she became Bets to one and all.

Since Papa's arrest, she had worked side by side with Mary to keep everything clean and manage the ever-dwindling food supply. She tried to corral Jake and care for Thomas, while Elizabeth spent her days meeting with the constables and trying to arrange meetings with the magistrates. Had the pressure been too much for Bets?

"Mary, are you listening to me?" Bets asked, shaking her for emphasis. "Why didn't you wake Jake to go with you?"

"I did just fine by myself," Mary replied, her exasperation growing. "Jake's only seven years old. He needs his sleep."

"Did you not think that he might have sped your journey? For Elizabeth's sake?" Bets's voice was shrill.

"Well, no. I never considered—"

"And did you not think that it might have helped Elizabeth to have someone sit with her?" Bets asked, continuing to pace. Mary could hear the boys stirring upstairs.

"I was in a hurry." Her sister was right. "Perhaps I was not thinking clearly." She had spent so many years trying to conquer her fears, maybe she had become too self-reliant— but then, had Papa not asked her to take care of the family? "It was the first time I was able to help Elizabeth alone. Truly help. It felt good to be the one bringing aid to Elizabeth," Mary confessed, surprising herself with the admission.

Bets's anger seemed to deflate. Her breathing slowed; she seemed to gain control for a moment, but the built-up tension exploded in tears.

"Forgive me for getting so angry." Bets was crying. "'Tis sometimes too much for me."

Mary moved closer to her sister and reached out to put an arm around her. This time the gesture was not rejected.

"I just don't know how we are to get on," sobbed Bets. "We have no way of earning a living. Elizabeth is ill now and she's the one who must see to father's release. Jake is getting to be a regular rogue. Much of the time I don't know where he is . . . he could be running with that group of young ruffians." Bets was sobbing.

"You cannot start worrying now, little sister. You are my brick—as solid as they come." Mary took a square of neatly hemstitched Irish linen from inside the sleeve of her *chemise* and reached out to wipe the young girl's face.

Bets laughed weakly. "It's hard to stay mad at someone who tries to wipe tears from your ears." She guided Mary's handkerchief to her eyes. "So, tell me, wise sister, whatever are we to do?"

"Why not follow your own recipe? Leave tomorrow's problems for tomorrow. Doesn't Papa's Bible even tell us, 'Sufficient unto the day is the evil thereof'?" Mary could tell from the tenseness in Bets's shoulders that she needed more encouragement than that, but when it came to encouragement from the Bible, Mary was not the one to give it. *Oh, why are things in such a muddle? Why is Papa not here to make everything better?*

"Very well," Mary lowered her voice, "I shall tell you a

secret. I am close to lighting upon the perfect plan to keep salt on our table and fresh thatch over our heads." Mary hoped it wasn't obvious that she was making this tale up as she spoke. "More than that, I cannot say right now. Just trust me for a few more days."

"Hallo?" Both girls heard the midwife's call at the same time. "Mary? Bets?"

"Aye, Midwife Dunkirk. We're coming," answered Mary. They made their way into the common room. From the tone of the midwife's voice, the news was not good.

"We lost the little one, but young Elizabeth will live." The woman didn't temper her news. Throughout the *shire*, she was known for her plain speaking. "Would ye like to see yer stepmama? Mind now, 'twill not be good to overtire her." The sisters assured her that they would make their visit a short one.

Not knowing what to say to Elizabeth, Mary only knew that for the first time, she needed to be near her stepmother.

Elizabeth spoke first as they drew near to her bed. "I grieve that I have lost your little brother, but I trust he is in God's hands now." Mary felt Elizabeth tremble as their hands touched. "Mary, thank you for bringing Midwife Dunkirk to help me. You are so very brave." She also spoke to Bets. "And I thank you for staying with me. How frightening it was until you came to be by my side." Her voice sounded frail from exhaustion. "'Tis a great loss, but 'twould be so much harder to bear would it not be for having four dear children already."

Mary realized that Elizabeth never used the word *step* when referring to the Bunyan children.

Smoothing down Mary's curls, Elizabeth said, "I had hoped the little one would have springy curls like you, Mary."

Mary felt that lump rising in her throat again.

"And I do love the soft gold of your hair, but I confess I was wishing to see Bets's coppery color on the babe."

Mary felt Elizabeth shift toward the cradle that had been placed between the bed and the far wall by Papa before his arrest. A tiny linen-wrapped bundle must be lying there, waiting for burial.

"Would he have had blue eyes, Elizabeth?" Bets asked. Mary could have kicked her sister's shin had she any idea where to aim.

"Most likely, though being my first child, it is hard to be certain."

Elizabeth was beginning to sound drowsy. "We hardly know any other color in this Bunyan clan, though Bets's eyes seem more green than blue most days." She squeezed Mary's hand. "Now, Mary, do not be impatient with Bets. I know you think 'twould be better not to mention the little one, but I tell you truth, it surely does help to talk about him."

"It doesn't hurt too much?" Mary wanted to be sure.

"No. I've learned that grieving is harder when 'tis not shared." Elizabeth's voice seemed to fade. "I do wish your father were here."

The midwife took Mary's hand, indicating that they should let Elizabeth rest. "Ye girls must lie down and try to get some sleep before yer young brothers get up."

Elizabeth was drifting off. "We will have to get word to John."

They helped the Dunkirks gather their things and load their baskets. Mary knew Bets would be tucking some of Elizabeth's tart apple *pommage* into the basket as well.

The midwife recited a litany of instructions to them. "Do not let those boys tire her. Get word to me if she becomes *peaky* or feverish. Make sure she rests. Dunkirk will be back on the morrow to help bury the little one. And worry not about my fee. Yer father's congregation will take care of it."

Mary grimaced, wishing she had the coin to pay the midwife then and there.

As soon as the horse-drawn cart rolled away, Bets checked on Elizabeth one last time, then the sisters made their way upstairs to catch what little slumber was left to them. It had been an exhausting night.

As they drifted off to sleep, Bets turned to Mary and said, "I am so thankful you told me that you have a plan. Now I will not have as much to worry about." She rolled over. "Good night, Mary."

"Good night, Bets."

*The plan.* She was relieved that the quarrel was over, but now she must come up with the plan she had promised Bets—any plan. Mary was too tired to worry about it. *I-can-do-all-things . . . I-can-do-all-things . . . but I am ever so glad I can do them tomorrow.*

# 4
# Slough
# of Despond

M ary."

"Ummm."

"Mary, it's way past dawn."

Mary could feel Bets gently shaking her. "I'm so tired."

"We've only been asleep for a few hours, but Thomas woke crying. He's cutting teeth again." Bets sounded weary. "I didn't want him to wake Elizabeth. She's still sleeping."

"Elizabeth is still sleeping and it's after dawn?" Mary asked, still groggy.

"Mary." Bets was getting impatient. "Don't you remember that she lost the baby in the night?"

Mary sat up. "Oh, Bets, how could I have forgotten? I'm sorry I didn't wake up with Thomas."

"It's no wonder you are so tired. You walked all the way to get the midwife." Bets bustled around the loft, tidying the boys' *pallets*.

"Where is Jake? Why are you making his bed?"

"He took off early this morning. I'm not really making his bed, it's just that—"

"Bets, I can hear exactly what you are doing. Did he say where he was going?" Mary scooted over to where Bets was kneeling and put her hands on her sister's shoulders. She felt the tenseness of the muscles. It was difficult to hide feelings from Mary's sensitive fingers.

"No."

"But you are worried, aren't you?" Mary asked.

"Yes." Bets exhaled long and slowly. Her shoulders dropped. "I don't know what to do about Jake. I needed him to take soup to Papa and now he's gone. I don't want Elizabeth worrying about Papa on top of everything else. The Dunkirks said that they would see that the arrangements are made for the baby's burial, but it will take all of Elizabeth's strength to do it."

"When did they say they would come?" Mary helped Bets smooth the boys' bedcovers. It went twice as fast when they worked together.

"The midwife didn't say. But with Thomas so fussy, I can't leave." Bets moved over to their own bed and began straightening the blankets.

Mary took her *pantalets* off the shelf and balanced on one leg and then the other as she pulled them on. She quickly cinched the drawstring, securing it at the waist, then reached for her woolen dress hanging on the peg nearby. She pulled it over her *chemise*, tying all the laces. Next came a fresh apron, then a woolen vest, which was laced tightly. She reached under her pillow, found Mama's blue ribbon, and slipped it into her apron pocket. "Of course you can't leave. Where is Thomas now?"

"He woke so early that he fell back asleep downstairs. To be safe, I tied his *leading strings* to the leg of the table." Bets chuckled. "I knew we would hear the movement of the table long before he could get into any mischief."

"You should have wakened me earlier." Mary finished straightening the loft. "How long have you been up?"

"Long enough to start the soup. With all the comings and goings today, I knew we'd need a well-stocked soup pot, with enough to take a hearty meal to Papa."

"Oh, Bets," Mary said, hugging her sister, "what would I ever do without you?"

"You'd be as lost as I would be without you. Now let's put our heads together and decide what to do."

"I'll take the soup to Papa." Mary didn't wait for Bets to protest. They both knew there was no alternative. "How I hate to tell him about Elizabeth and the baby."

"I will stay here and see to Elizabeth and Thomas. The bread must be baked first so that we can offer a meal when the Dunkirks come. People from Papa's congregation might also stop in." Bets grabbed Mary's hands. "I wasn't worried about using the last of the eggs and the milk to make a light custard for Elizabeth, thanks to you."

"To me?" Mary didn't understand.

"Yes, you goose." Bets tugged one of Mary's curls playfully. "Because of your plan."

Mary had forgotten all about the plan.

"This morning, as I was cooking, I decided to make you tell me the whole plan—every single detail."

Mary sensed excitement through Bets's fingers. "You did?"

"Yes, but then I remembered how much you like to work things out on your own." Bets paused. "Remember how angry I was last night when I said that you think you can do everything all by yourself?"

"Yes. You don't often get that mad. I'll not soon forget last night."

"Well, I was right. Oh, not in the mean way it came out, but I realized there was truth in what I said. You *can* do just about anything by yourself."

Mary loved hearing those words. "Thank you for that, Bets."

"So, I decided to let you surprise me with the plan. I know it will work out and I need not worry again about how we are to survive while Papa is away."

The plan. *What have I done?* Mary thought. *I have to come up with a plan.*

"By the time Elizabeth is well she can put her energy toward getting Papa released, and not have to worry about how we are to put food on the table." Bets hugged Mary. Her voice sounded lighter than any time since Papa's arrest.

Mary was glad for the load lifted off her sister, but her own burden now weighed heavily. She welcomed Bets's faith in her, but could she live up to her rash promises? What kind of plan could she devise?

And where was Jake? Bets was worried. Since Papa's arrest Jake was a lost soul. Mary knew he missed Papa. She also knew he hated, as he so often said, "being surrounded by women." Bets was probably right that he was in danger of being led astray by Gifre and his cronies. Tonight, she would just have to lay down the law to Jake. Yes, she was worried too.

⁂

Mary made her way once again through the streets of Bedford. It was midday, though the only difference to Mary was the welcome warmth of the late autumn sun and the bustle of traffic on Mill Lane. The Bunyan cottage was a little more than two *furlongs* from Bedford *Gaol*.

Mary's cane tapped out the cobbled rhythm of the road. She passed to the right of the *plat* that was so familiar. Sitting back from the road was the large barn called Dissenting Meeting—the name for her father's church. They used to meet in beautiful St. John's, but along with the *Restoration* came an eviction notice. *This barn suits our growing congregation,* Mary thought. She could not see it as she passed, but the sound of the late autumn wind whipping the branches of the ancient beech was as familiar to her as the songs that rang from the timbers of the meetinghouse every Sunday.

"Hallo, Mary."

"Good day to you, Elder Owens." Mary recognized the citizens of Bedford easily by their voices. Many she distinguished by their footfall or their scent.

"I am heading over to see your stepmama. How is she faring?"

"She is tired and sad, but the midwife says that she will recover. Will you be saying words over the baby?"

"Aye. With your father in prison, I am trying to care for the congregation as best I can."

"I'll tell Papa. He'll be so glad to hear."

"Are you heading there now, Mary?"

"Yes, we are to bring midday meal each day." Mary lifted the jug of soup. She had a cloth knotted over her arm, cradling a warm loaf of Bets's bread. Bets wanted to put a small crock of custard in the cloth as well, but Mary told her it would not fare well next to the warm loaf. The truth was that she was afraid her father would think they were being lavish with supplies. If he saw so much food offered at one meal, he would be concerned. Until Mary had a plan, she needed to be cautious.

"Tell your Papa we are praying for him."

"Aye."

"How is the family faring?" The elder coughed slightly, enough to let Mary know he was embarrassed to ask. He, as well as the rest of the congregation, had a hard enough time feeding their own children. She also knew that they must have taken up a collection to pay for the midwife and the burial costs for the baby.

"Thank you for asking, Elder." Mary tried to muster a confident voice. "We are getting along fine, so far." Before he could question her further, she said, "I'll need to be on my way before the soup cools."

"Good day, Mary."

*I hate being poor. I hate being frightened. I hate having Papa in prison. I hate* . . . Her litany was interrupted by a sound behind her. Faintly, she heard two sets of footsteps, one with the extra slap of a loose sole. "Jake?"

Nothing. She listened as hard as she could and finally she heard the sound of them running off. Could that have been

Jake? Why would he hide his identity from her? Who was with him? *Oh, Papa, how we need you at home!*

Mary continued to make her way to the Bedford *Gaol.*

Mary knocked on the jailer's door. After a time, he opened the door to let her in. The jailer was a quiet fellow, but Mary knew that he had befriended her father. The key rasped into the padlock and she listened for the resolute clicks of the tumbler. The bolt jammed against the door hasp and she heard the creak of the bolt arm turning. The heavily studded door groaned as it opened. Mary knew the jailer must be a sturdy fellow to open this door several times each day.

The overwhelming stench of slop buckets jolted Mary's sensitive nose. She knew from the intense odor that they were not emptied regularly. That mingled with the stink of unwashed bodies and sickness and mildewed straw. If the door had not been locked after her, Mary would have turned around and left. Her heart hammered as if she had run the whole way.

She reached into her pocket to pull a sprig off the rosemary she always carried. Crushing it to release the powerful scent, she put her hand by her nose. *Ahhh. Better.*

"Papa?" With so much rustling and movement in the room, she didn't dare move out lest she stumble over someone.

"Bunyan, yer little girl is here," said a voice from the room.

"Mary?"

The voice she loved so well! Strong arms wrapped around her, carrying her over to his place.

"Oh, wee Mary, you don't know how beautiful you look. I'm sorry I didn't see you at first, but I was sleeping. I have been having the most extraordinary dreams." Papa put her down on a box near a bed of straw. He sat on something and pulled it close to Mary so that they touched.

"I brought you some of Bets's soup, Papa. And a loaf of freshly baked bread."

"Thank you, little daughter. 'Tis most welcome, but not as welcome as your sweet face."

She gave him the crock with soup and slid the knotted cloth off her arm. Papa put his hand underneath to support it while she untied it. Inside was a spoon and the small loaf of bread. "Eat while it is still warm. I need to take the empty crock and spoon back with me."

"I'd rather just visit with you, but we don't want Bets to feel that her gift was not appreciated, do we?" He took a spoonful, slurping a little so that Mary knew he liked it. It was an old routine from the days when she was small and would bring him a pretend bowl of soup.

"Ummm. This is good. Hearty. Give our little Bets my thanks. Don't bring the bread next time. I doubt not that I will enjoy this home-baked loaf, but they provide each prisoner a quarter loaf of *maslin* each day. I must pay a half-*groat* each month whether I take it or not."

"Papa, are you well?"

"Hmm, yes," he said between spoons of soup. "I have the constitution of an ox. It will stand me in good stead here in prison. Thanks be to God you are hearty too, or I could not

46

allow you to visit me." He paused. "This place is not a good place for the weak or the infirm." He gave her back the crock and spoon and helped her tie them into the cloth. "Now tell me about my precious Elizabeth and the family." He tore off a piece of bread, releasing a yeasty odor.

"I have bad news, Papa." Mary could feel that familiar lump lodge in her throat. *Don't cry, Mary. Don't cry.*

"What, Mary?" Papa put down the bread and took both her hands. "Tell me child, what is it?" Mary could hear the rising fear in his voice.

"Elizabeth lost the baby last night."

"Oh, Father, be with Elizabeth . . ."

Mary knew her father wasn't speaking to her. He was talking to his heavenly Father. *A lot of good that does now,* Mary thought. *The time God could have helped was before Elizabeth lost the little one.* She would never say that to her Father, though. He seemed to believe that God was always in control, even when horrible things happened, like jail or death. Mary did not understand.

"Tell me everything, Mary."

She told her father everything—from how she went to get the midwife all the way to the little bundle that would be buried today. He was silent. Mary had to know, so she put her hands to his face. She could feel the wetness. Papa took both her hands and kissed the palms.

"I smell rosemary."

Mary sensed his struggle to gain control. This room was filled with prisoners. Although her father was never shy about showing emotions, she knew he would want to grieve in solitude. "Yes. Does it not smell good?"

"Rosemary for remembrance." He used to repeat the old rhymes to her when she was little. "I can never smell rosemary without thinking of you."

Mary took the sprigs of rosemary out of her pocket and gave them to her father. "You can remember me and keep from smelling bad odors, all at the same time."

"Thank you, wee Mary." Crushing a stem of rosemary, he breathed deeply. "Your news reminds me of a part of my dream. It concerned a pilgrim who undertook a journey to escape the destruction of his village."

"Did his family journey with him?" asked Mary.

"No, sadly, they did not." He was silent so long that Mary feared he would leave the rest of the story untold.

"Where was he journeying?" Mary asked.

"His ultimate destination was the Celestial City. But that was far in the future. Early on, he conversed with a fellow traveler and paid no attention to the narrow path." Papa tickled her. "He did not have your ability to feel the pathway with his feet."

"Oh, Papa." It was good to hear him teasing her again.

"He only traveled a short distance when he stumbled into a swamp. Mired in mud, he flailed around, but to no avail. His companion realized this was no pleasure trip and managed to get out of the bog and head back to the City of Destruction."

"Was that the town the pilgrim came from?"

"Yes."

"Why was the companion able to get out while Pilgrim could not?"

"The companion took the easy way out—back the way they had come. Pilgrim was not willing to go backward. He was weighted down by a heavy burden on his back. Knowing the burden would be lifted somewhere ahead, he continued to struggle forward."

"How did he get out?"

"Help came along."

"What kind of help?" Mary couldn't stop asking questions. She loved her father's stories.

"Nay. Help was the name of the man. He reached down and pulled the pilgrim out of the slough. Help told him the name of the bog was Slough of Despond."

"Despond? Like grief or sadness?"

"Aye."

"'Tis a good thing Help came along. Right, Papa? 'Tis too bad the pilgrim could not climb out on his own."

"Sometimes in life, help will not come along. Had Pilgrim but known it, steps were placed throughout the Slough of Despond to guide him out of the mire. He did not know how to find them."

"So, he could have done it all by himself!" A note of triumph crept into Mary's voice.

"Well, he may have thought so, wee Mary, but the steps were provided by the King." Papa continued to hold her hands. "This story from my dream is called an allegory. Do you remember what an allegory is?"

"'Tis like the parables in the Bible, where the story has a deeper meaning."

"Aye. The steps provided by the King were the promises that God gave us in the Bible."

"So when we must escape our swamps—our troubles— we need to use God's promises instead of our own strength?"

"I know 'tis hard to believe, my stubborn little Mary, but in due time . . . in due time." He lifted Mary up in his arms. "Do you enjoy being lifted high, little daughter? 'Tis one thing you cannot do on your own."

Mary could not help but giggle.

"I want you to remember who helps you out of bogs. It is found in the second verse of David's fortieth Psalm—'He,' meaning our heavenly Father, 'brought me up also out of an horrible pit, out of the miry clay, and set my feet upon a rock, and established my goings.'"

Mary settled back into his lap when he sat down again. "What made you think of the Slough of Despond, Papa?"

"As you told me of our losing the babe and as I thought of the pain Elizabeth endures without me, I felt myself getting sucked into the quicksand of despondence." He reached over and took something off the table by his stool. "I thank God that I have this book with me." He placed his well-used Bible into Mary's hands. She loved the softness of the worn leather binding. "In here are the steps to guide me out of the mire once again." He took the Bible from her hands.

The scent of rosemary told Mary that he pressed her sprigs into the pages of his Bible before putting it back.

As Mary walked home, she thought about her father's last question for her. "What swamp are you struggling to escape, Mary?"

*How I would love to lay all my fears at Papa's feet. I wish I could tell him about our worry over Jake and that we will soon be out of money. But all I think about is the wetness on his face and the droop of his shoulders as I sat on his lap. You have burden enough, dear Papa. I must do this on my own.*

Deep in thought, she hardly noticed the round pebbles underfoot, and before she could help herself, she was slipping and skidding. She lifted the cloth with the empty soup crock to keep it from breaking. She fell to the cobbles, the force jarring her teeth.

Was that Gifre she heard, snickering in the distance? She was almost certain. She ran her fingers across the ground all around her. Small pebbles had been sprinkled across the path. It was a deliberate prank.

Just then Mary heard a sound that froze her thoughts—the sound of a loose sole beating out a familiar rhythm as someone ran in the opposite direction.

Mary picked herself up and felt inside the knotted cloth to make sure the soup crock hadn't broken. *Good,* she thought. *At least Papa's mug is safe. I'll not even think about what I think I heard. Jake would not be part of this. I must be imagining things.*

She resumed her trek home. *Now on to a plan. I must make my way out of this swamp. I-can-do-all-things . . . I-can-do-all-things . . .*

## 5
# St. Andrew's Day Fair

*J*ake, please do not pull me." Mary was tired of stumbling after an excited seven year old.

Bets stayed home to care for Elizabeth and Thomas and to make soup. Once that was cooked, she wanted to scrub the floors. Mary felt guilty taking Jake, who could have eased Bets's workload by doing some of the harder tasks, but she wanted to keep him close today.

"We hafta hurry! I can hear music. I can smell the boiled pike!" Jake trembled with excitement, every muscle tensed like a tightly coiled spring.

Mary smelled more than boiled fish. The pungent odor of burning *peat* hung in the air, its acrid smokiness stinging her eyes. The warmth warded off the November chill, so the fair goers ignored the smoky pall.

She also smelled unwashed bodies. Since it was almost winter, most citizens of Bedfordshire would see no soap and water until late spring when the streams began to warm.

Elizabeth stubbornly insisted that the Bunyans bathe every week. It was a strange practice, but Mary had gotten used to a level of cleanliness unusual among the people of Bedford. Jake always complained bitterly as they carried water to be heated and filled the tub near the warm stove. Elizabeth rigged hangings for privacy. Papa would bathe first, then Elizabeth. Mary was next, followed by Bets, and then a kicking, screaming Jake was hauled in. By the time they got to Baby Thomas, the water was so dirty that Papa would tease, "Don't throw the baby out with the bathwater."

Washing outer garments was as rare as bathing for most. Everyone knew that too much washing would wear the clothing out long before its time. Everyone except Elizabeth, that is. Clothing in the Bunyan home was scrubbed religiously. It was said that no one in the *shire* could get underclothing and nightgowns as white as Elizabeth Bunyan. Mary was glad. She loved the clean, sunshiny smell of her clothing. She once heard the neighboring women pass by their yard, making clucking noises. They couldn't understand this finicky young Elizabeth.

Clean clothes were not a point of pride, however, with most of the crowds jostling Mary and Jake today. Mary pulled a sprig of rosemary from her pocket and crushed it between her fingers, releasing the fragrance. Each time her sensitive nose protested, she raised her hand to her nostrils and once again let the rosemary scent drown the pungent smells of the crowd. She recalled her father saying, "Rosemary for remembrance."

She remembered why she was here—to come up with a plan.

"Jake, what do you see?"

"Animals and people." He squirmed and twisted.

"'Tis not a lot of help." She squeezed his fingers impatiently.

Mary caught the distinctive scents of the animals. There were probably more animals than people here. Fairs took place all across the British Isles. Bedford had four fairs every year—one in June, another in August, the St. Matthew's Day Fair in September, and this last fair of the year on St. Andrew's Day, November 30th. People came from all over Bedford and neighboring towns to buy and sell their animals, produce, and wares.

Mary heard the bawl of cows mixed with the clang of cowbells. Cowbells always reminded her of Papa. He fancied casting the big iron bells.

Cows were not the only animals at the fair. She heard the rustle of doves' wings against the wire of their *dovecote*. When they settled down, she caught the clear coo-coo-coo of their talk.

Could doves be the answer to their problem? She wished there were time to sit alongside and overhear their cooing. The *dovecote* was a fascinating community. She pretended the doves were talking about her. If she listened long enough, would she come to understand what they were saying? She pushed her finger between the wires. If she was very still, one might come close to investigate and she could rub the soft, feathery down of his head.

"What ya doing, Mary?" Jake pulled her out of her reverie.

"I wonder if we could raise doves to make money."

"Naw, there's not much meat in doves, so they only sell for a penny apiece."

"Meat?" Mary was horrified. "You mean they raise these gentle birds for meat?"

"Sure. Gif—I mean, my friend tried to raise them to make money and finally gave up on the whole thing. He ended up with chickens. Besides, where would you get the money to buy the first pair?"

"Hmmm. I guess you are right, Jake. 'Tis not for us." She pulled herself away from the *dovecote*.

Her feet told of the bustle of the fair. She could feel the quiver in the ground that bespoke a herd of sheep on the move. As they got closer she picked out the staccato bark of the sheepdogs, the sharp commands of the shepherd, and the bleating of sheep. The smell of dust and sheep mingled as the herd moved on. She sensed, by the bustle of activity, that the St. Andrew's Day Fair was far more exciting than a mere market day. The wriggling young hand holding hers told her that Jake felt the excitement too.

"I smell good food and I hear music up ahead."

"You know I smell and hear just fine, Master John Bunyan, the Younger. Please, tell me what you *see!*"

"Aw, Mary, 'tis too much to tell." He was practically squirming. "And don't use my whole name. I hate it when you say my name all the way through the *younger*."

"Please." She hungered for details. "Tell me what it looks like."

"*'Swounds!* I'm sick of having to look at everything for you." He wriggled impatiently. "I want to *do,* not just to see."

"You watch your language! If you want to talk about Jesus' wounds, you do it before Papa. He would be so disappointed to hear you. You know what a time he had ridding his own language of profanity in his youth. How he would hate to see you take up the habit."

Mary wished she could see Jake. Did his face show penitence? She missed much of the subtle information that came from watching faces. If Bets were not around to see for her, she could only listen for it in the voice.

"I don't even know why I came with you." Jake's voice was almost a whine. "This is no fun. If I have to spend my time making words for you, 'twould be better had I stayed home with Bets."

"You can be such a beast, Jake." She gave his arm a jerk for emphasis. "We are here to solve a problem, not to have fun." Brothers were hardly worth the work sometimes. "You *have* to help me."

"Awright." His reluctance showed in his voice. "Just ahead of us is a squire talking to his lady."

"What do they look like?"

"The lady is dressed real fancy with big skirts." He whistled. "She must have a hunnerd petticoats on."

"She couldn't have a hundred."

"Well, it looks like it. Every one o' them is dragging in the dirt."

Mary laughed. Now this was a picture!

"You know what's funny, Mary?"

"What?"

"The squire is dressed fancier than his lady."

"Tell me."

"Well . . . she is dressed in a sort of dull color, not much different from chicken splat."

"Jake!"

"You asked for a picture, Mary. You want me to go on or not?"

Mary laughed. "Go on, Jake. I guess I did ask you to give me a picture."

"An' he's dressed in a jacket the color of . . . umm . . . sunset in late summer. You know, when the dust of harvest turns it orangey red." He paused. "He's got little thread squiggles all over his waistcoat."

"Thread squiggles? Oh, you mean embroidery."

"Yes. Embroidery. An' he has more 'n a hunnerd silver buttons on his jacket."

"Jake?"

"I'm not joshing, Mary. He has 'em running up and down the front of his waistcoat, holding up his cuffs, on his jacket. Everywhere."

"Buttons, huh?" Could Papa make buttons in prison? He had mentioned that many prisoners crafted things in order to support their families. Where could she get money to buy silver? And how could he heat the metal to pour into molds? They didn't even have the heat of a fireplace in the prison, let alone a place to set up a small forge. No, buttons would never work.

"Do you want to hear more or not?" Jake hated to be ignored.

"I'm sorry, Jake, I was thinking. Please go on."

"She wears a funny little cap, but his is a tall-crowned hat with a huge feather that curls in toward his face."

"Those are called ostrich plumes. Can you picture the bird who once wore those?"

Jake giggled. "And he wears ribbons everywhere—tied

in bows at the cuff of his breeches—around his waist. They even dangle from the skirt of his jacket."

"Why is it that when he moves, he makes a tinkling sound?"

"'Cause every one of those laces has a metal tip."

"Father would have called him a *popinjay,* wouldn't he, Jake?"

Jake laughed as the couple moved off, probably never realizing they were the subject of such close scrutiny.

Mary couldn't stop thinking of those ribbons. She continued to play that tinkling sound in her memory.

When Mary realized that the fair was in town, she knew she must investigate. Although pretty sure Elizabeth would have forbidden it, she had committed herself by telling Bets she had a plan to feed the family. Now she had to make her wish into truth. She must come up with something and she was not about to apply for help from the parish!

Because of her blindness, she was certainly eligible for help. Everyone knew well the three categories of poverty. The law specified that the orphan, the blind, the aged, the lame, and the incurably diseased belonged to one class, which they called "poor by impotency." Just the name made Mary's stomach clench. There was hardly a word she hated more than the word *poor.*

The second class, the "poor by casualty," included wounded soldiers and the sick. Both of these classes made up the Parish Poor and could apply for help from the state church. The church squeezed the money out of the parishioners with the poor tax, collected each week. Mary knew that the parish-ioners hated the poor, no matter what class, because of that poor tax. She was not about to put her hand in their pockets! They could just keep their baskets of moldy bread and their rags. *If that be pride, then I shall be judged guilty,* Mary fumed inwardly. *Better to be prideful than to resign myself to living with "poor blind Mary."*

The third category of the poor crowded the St. Andrew's Day Fair. Mary heard the roll of dice on the top of overturned barrels. She caught snatches of *minstrel* song. She knew the *jongleurs* were juggling their leather balls and the fortune-tellers plying their tricks. These were the "thriftless poor." It was against the law to be poor by choice.

No doubt about it—England dealt harshly with these folk. The first time arrested they were whipped and a hole was burned through the *gristle* of their ear. Then they were sentenced to work for a whole year on the land of one of the leading citizens. If they were caught idle a second time, the other ear was burnt and they were sentenced to a second year's servitude. The law offered no third chances. If they were caught again they were hung. The saying was well known —"you can only beg food until the *gallows* devour you." *Nay, there is no protection for the penniless.*

"Can you describe the wares to me, Jake?" Mary asked. "Tell me what the people look like, what they are selling, what kind of people are . . ."

"Oh, look, Mary! There's a man with a dancing bear. You stay right here. I'll be back. I hafta go." Jake dropped Mary's hand.

"Jake! You must not go. Come back!"

Mary sensed emptiness where he had been standing. That boy! She should have been pleased at this proof that her brother believed in her ability to fend for herself, but somehow she just felt frightened.

She reached out her hand and cautiously took a step forward just as a group of whirling, laughing children parted to run around her. Tipped off balance, she landed on hands and knees in the dirt. *Don't cry . . . Don't cry . . . I can do all things . . . I . . .*

# An Unusual Friendship

*hey?* Are you all right?" A girl's voice.

"I am fine. My brother ran off to watch a dancing bear and forgot all about me."

"I watched." The voice had an interesting sound, as if the tongue lingered on the roof of the mouth and then drew out the last syllable. The *w* sounded almost like *v*.

"You called me *Chey,* but my name is Mary." She sat down right where she had fallen.

"My name is Sofia, and I already know who you are. You are the blind daughter of the Elstow tinker, Bunyan. My father also is a tinker." Sofia seemed to pause. "We are *Rom.*" When she said *Rom,* the *r* rumbled ever so slightly. The intensity of her words as they rolled around her mouth made her words so different from the plain talk Mary was used to.

"*Rom?*" Mary asked.

"You *gadje* call us gypsies. We speak *Romani. Chey* is our word for girl." Sofia was very still. "Do you want me to get you some help and then leave?"

"I do not need help," Mary answered automatically, missing the hesitation in Sofia's voice.

"I understand. It is hard to be pitied, no?" said Sofia matter-of-factly.

"How do you know about pity? Are you infirm?" Mary was intrigued.

"No, worse. We are *Rom*."

"I do not understand."

"Many *gadje* despise the *Rom*. Since you do not despise Sofia, then let me show you the way to my *kumpania*. There we can sit while we talk. I will ask my brothers to look for your Jake." Sofia's touch was tentative on Mary's shoulder.

"Thank you, Sofia. Let me get up and shake off this dirt."

Mary stood and brushed off as much of her dress as she could reach. Sofia brushed off the rest, then took Mary's hand and gently guided her around the obstacle course that was the St. Andrew's Day Fair in Bedford.

The air bristled with excitement. Now that she felt safe, Mary could smell savory tarts and hear rhythmic tinkling metal sounds. It reminded her of the man's ribbons. "Sofia, what is the jingling sound?"

"That," said Sofia, "is part of my *kumpania*—my family. Those are the *boria*, my sisters-in-law, Aziza and Jamila. They are dancing."

"Dancing?" Mary wasn't sure dancing was the kind of activity Papa would approve.

"Not the kind of dancing you think, *Gadje*." Sofia laughed. "This is not dancing with men. This is the *borias'* job. They lay a red silken scarf on the ground, and if their dances please, people throw pennies or perhaps a half-*groat* on the scarf."

"Sofia, help me see it!" The request slipped out before Mary could stop herself. She hated to ask for help, but she hungered for word pictures. She also wanted to know about the pennies. After all, that was why she had come to the fair. She had to come up with some kind of plan to earn money!

"Of course, *Gadje Chey*. A gypsy likes nothing better than to tell a story. First you must sit here, and then—"

"But wait." Mary held up her hand. "What is *gadje* and what is *kumpania?* You told me that *chey* meant girl; what do the other words mean?"

Sofia laughed again. Mary loved to hear Sofia's laugh. It was full of gentle humor and good nature, and made her realize that laughs could mean all kinds of things. Some people laughed when they were nervous, a kind of tittering laugh. There was the kind of laughter that exploded out of people in a loud guffaw of happiness. Others laughed from evilness, like Gifre when he was tormenting her. She imagined his wicked snickering every time she felt frightened and unprotected.

"Mary, didn't you just ask me a question?" Sofia laughed again.

"I am sorry." Mary blushed. "My mind went wandering."

"*Gadje* means someone who is not *Rom*. It means you are not a gypsy. *Kumpania* means my family."

"How many people in your family, Sofia?"

"Hundreds." Sofia laughed her wonderful laugh again. "*Kumpania* really means bands of families who travel together across the countryside." Sofia guided Mary to an upturned wooden crate. "Sit here for a minute. I'll be right back."

Mary heard a jumble of sounds. Slowly she picked out familiar sounds—the cackle of chickens flapping against a crate and the fishmonger singing out his wares in a melodious singsong: "Eels, fresh eels. Haddock too. Sprat 'n' cod 'n' pike for you!"

The mournful sound of a violin reminded her of Papa. Papa loved music so much that when Mary was small he made a violin out of iron. It took him most of a year to finish. Mary loved the coolness of the metal, the delicate cutwork scrolls, and the intricate fretwork of the bridge. Papa was such a talented tinker, such a gifted metalsmith, that Mary could run her hands over the entire violin without ever feeling a rough spot or sharpness.

Friends laughed when Papa brought out this instrument, thinking he had fashioned it only as an oddity. But when he drew the bow across the strings the sound made Mary's heart ache. Papa said it was only an earthly substitute for the music of the angels, but it made Mary want to catch the sound in her hands and throw it to the winds. Other times she wanted to gather the swirling music and keep it forever.

Today the sound of the violin just made Mary sad. *Oh, Papa. I must not forget what I came to do. I must find some way to feed our family until you come home. Come home. Those words sound so good, but seem so impossible. Papa, I miss you.*

"I'm back, Mary." Sofia sat down on the crate next to Mary. "Here, I brought you a treat." She placed a twist of paper in Mary's hand. "Open it."

Mary untwisted the end of the paper. She could tell by the

shape and stickiness that Sofia had brought her a piece of *marchpane* and two *suckets*. "Oh, Sofia. Candy! I have not had candy in ever so long."

"*I Puri Daj*, the old mother, sent these for you. She will talk stories to you later."

"I shall thank her," said Mary. "Please take one of the *suckets* and we'll share the *marchpane*." Mary broke the piece in two and gave half to Sofia. Biting off a small piece of *marchpane*, she let the sweetness of almonds sit on her tongue. "Now tell me about your family and about the fair, please."

Sofia sucked on her candy as she talked. "My family are travelers. We have no home, but go from place to place in our caravans."

It reminded Mary of a verse her father read to her from the Bible—*The foxes have holes, and the birds of the air have nests; but the Son of man hath nowhere to lay his head.*

"I wish you could see our wagons. They are much more beautiful than houses. Ours is painted red like the color that drips off summer strawberries."

Mary could taste the sweetness and warmth of that color. "Oh, Sofia, I love red."

"*I Puri Daj* is the best artist in our *kumpania*. She takes colors—the cool winter sky, bittersweet, saffron, the pink of the musk rose—and swirls them into the most beautiful designs. *O Puro Dad*, my grandfather, makes a varnish from the resin of trees and linseed oil. He cooks it over the fires for days until it is clear like water, then adds turpentine. Every year he paints this over our wagon to protect *I Puri Daj's* decoration. It shines so clear, it sparkles in the sunlight."

"I can almost see it." Mary could feel the chill air; the

crispness had a strong bite to it. She pulled her cloak tighter. "The blue must be strong against the delicate musk rose."

"Oh, Mary! You can see it."

Mary was thankful that Sofia had found her. Here was someone who could make word pictures like Papa. "Don't stop, Sofia. I want to hear everything."

Sofia's bubbling laughter filled the air around Mary. "My *kumpania's* caravan follows the fairs all over the isle of Britain. My uncle is master of the dancing bear. My *daj*—I mean my mother—sells lanterns my *dad* makes. I told you that he is a tinker like your father."

"My Papa stopped his metalsmith work about four years ago," Mary said. "He is in Bedford *Gaol* now." Her stomach got that tight, lonely feeling again. "He is waiting for his trial. They arrested him for preaching without a license." Why was she telling all this to a stranger? "They say they will banish him."

"We know this, *Chey*. My *dad* hears the story of Friend Bunyan on the *Lungo Drom*."

"The *lungo drom?*" asked Mary.

"I forget you do not know *Romani. O Longo Drom* means the long road. It is the journey we make, the traveling of our *kumpania*." Sofia continued, "Uncle Timoz, he tells us about these sad events. He says that the *gadje* churchmen do not like *mechanick* preachers ."

Mary had heard all this before. "They are angry that men who work with their hands six days a week think they can preach on Sunday."

"Timoz says they are angry that so many people listen to your father. Uncle Timoz himself has heard your father preach and he says it makes him glad to hear about *Yeshua ben Miriam* from the lips of one who is *Yeshua's* friend."

"*Yeshua?*" asked Mary.

"You call him Jesus," Sofia explained. "Timoz says to see if we can help the Tinker's family."

"We don't need any help." Mary bit out the words almost before Sofia could finish her thought.

"Oh, so we are back to that, *Gadje Chey.*" Sofia laughed once again. "That's what's wrong with your people. You try to do everything alone." Mary started to protest, but this time Sofia kept right on talking. "The *Rom* know that we must depend on our *kumpania*. We must help each other." Sofia laughed, lightly tapping her index finger against Mary's cheek as she said, "You *gadje* . . ."

Mary caught the other girl's scent as she moved. It smelled exotic somehow, a faint blend of wood smoke and dried herbs.

"You are right, Sofia," Mary admitted. "I do hate to depend on other people for help. All my life it has been so."

"Timoz says—"

"Ouch!" Mary interrupted Sofia with a startled cry. Something stung her face. She reached up to rub the spot and felt a sticky wetness. Putting her fingers in her mouth, she recognized the metallic taste of blood. She felt another sharp sting catch the edge of her ear. What was it?

"Mary?" Sofia sounded puzzled.

"Ow!" This time something hit Mary's shoulder. She felt Sofia jump off the crate at the same time she heard a sound she would recognize anywhere—Gifre's evil snickering. Before she could say anything, she heard something that completely unsettled her—the muffled slap of a loose sole on the soft dirt.

## 7

# Gypsies, Beggars, and Tinkers

"Stop it, *Gadjo!*" Sofia screamed, moving in front of Mary. "Stop right now. Why do you shoot gravel at Mary Bunyan?"

"Are you talking to me, Gypsy scum?"

Mary was surprised by the transformation of her new friend as she stood, rigid with anger, between Mary and the voice that belonged to Gifre.

"Answer me, *Gadjo*-boy!"

Mary could hear a crowd begin to gather. "Sofia," she whispered, "leave him alone. He is dangerous." She didn't think Sofia heard her.

"Does it make you feel powerful, this tormenting of someone who doesn't fight back?" Sofia did not back down. "What has Mary ever done to harm you?"

Mary knew better than to goad Gifre. He was mean spirited in the best of times. What would he do now? She didn't have long to wonder.

"You keep out of it, Gypsy spawn!" Gifre spat the words into the air with as much force as the gravel he had earlier fired at Mary. "I'll not have the likes of you talking to me."

"I'll do more than talk if you torment Mary." Sofia was screaming as loudly as Gifre.

"Sofia, no!" Mary wished she could get them to stop. "Leave him be."

"That's right, Mary," Gifre yelled, "call your snarling dog off me."

"You leave Mary out of this!" Sofia yelled right back at him.

"You and Mary make a perfect pair—tinkers' daughters, the both of you," Gifre sneered. "Come to the fair to beg pennies? Shame, shame to you, Mary Bunyan! At least you picked another beggar to teach you how."

"Gifre, stop!" Mary covered her ears. She knew a crowd had gathered, and she was humiliated to be the center of such a scene. Could Jake be part of this crowd? No. Her brother would not stand idle while Gifre tormented them. Would he?

"What would your jailbird father think, Mary Bunyan, if he knew you were running with Christ-killers?" Gifre's voice took on a taunting tone. "Christ-killers, Christ-killers, begging, thieving Christ-killers." The singsong words faded as he ran away.

Mary heard the crowd slowly move off. She leaned forward to place her hands on Sofia's shoulders and felt a shudder go through the girl. "Sofia? Are you all right?"

Sofia didn't answer.

"Don't feel bad. He always says evil things. I don't know why he does this, but everyone knows they are not true," Mary reassured her friend.

Sofia seemed shaken by the things Gifre said. Mary felt the tenseness of her friend's shoulders. Why was Sofia so quiet? This silence was more menacing than her earlier anger.

Finally, Sofia exhaled a sigh that seemed to come from deep within. "What if the words of that *gadjo* are true, Mary?"

"What do you mean?"

"Not the beggar part or the charge of thievery. Long have we *Rom* learned to ignore those accusations." Sofia didn't seem bothered in the least by these. "And the only reason people look down on tinkers is because *Roma* have long practiced the profession. Tinkers, like your father, only share the scorn aimed at our people."

Mary didn't understand. "If you don't mind the things he said, why are you dismayed?"

"One accusation he made may very well be true, to our everlasting shame." Sofia's voice was barely audible. "I think we *are* Christ-killers."

Before Mary could respond, Sofia pulled her off the crate. "Come, Mary. Come see *I Puri Daj*. She will tell you the story while we wait for the men to find your brother."

<hr />

"So you are the tinker's daughter?"

Mary loved the deep rumble in the old woman's voice. Well-worn hands enveloped Mary's fingers. Calluses and a network of fine cracks told Mary that *I Puri Daj* had spent a lifetime working with her hands. Mary could tell that Sofia's *baba*—grandmother—was no longer as robust as she had once been. The blood pulsing in her wrist had not the rhythmic beat of youth, but her touch was light and sensitive. Mary knew that *I Puri Daj* could tell as much from Mary's hands as she was learning from the old woman's hands.

"I am honored you haf come to visit Sofia's old grand-mama." *I Puri Daj* seemed happy to meet Mary. "Sofia." She clapped her hands as if to summon a servant. "Bring a stool for Mary Bunyan." When she said Mary's name, it sounded like Meady Boonyan.

Bringing Mary's hands up to her face, she said, "Vould you like to see vhat I look like?" She laughed. "You haf ten eyes at the ends of your fingers. Never be afraid to use them." Instead of the *w* sound in *would* and *what,* she used a *v.* It sounded interesting to Mary's ears.

"Thank you, *I Puri Daj.* Sofia told me about you. I am honored to meet you." Mary delicately read the planes of the old woman's face with her hands. From the crinkles in the corners of her eyes, she knew that *I Puri Daj* laughed often. Missing were the worry lines and frown furrows that usually marked the forehead. The skin was dry, but not chapped by the cold November air. Mary liked this face. Her sensitive fingers told her that this face belonged to someone she could trust. "Thank you for letting me see you with my fingers as well."

"You, Mary Bunyan, know God's secret," *I Puri Daj* announced.

"I don't know any secret." Mary was puzzled.

"Never forget that you already know the secret . . . things ve see vith our eyes, they are temporal, they vill fade away. It is unseen things that vill last." She laughed.

Mary loved the sound of her laughter. "What does *temporal* mean?"

"Temporary, like dust under our vagons. It blows avay." She laughed again. "Vhen I paint my pictures, I try to capture the unseen things vith my brush. I do not do such a good job, I think."

Sofia was back with a stool for Mary. Sofia helped Mary sit, then plopped down on the ground next to her.

"So, tell me, Mary Bunyan, vhat can I do to help you?" *I Puri Daj* asked.

"Sofia says that her brothers can help me find Jake."

"Of course, of course." She flicked her fingers against Mary's hand in a dismissive gesture. "They already look for the boy. I mean, vhat can ve do to help vith problem that makes you look like you are pulling our whole caravan?"

Mary laughed at that picture. Her problems often seemed as weighty as the Gypsy caravans she'd felt pass by. Mary laughed so hard she ended up falling against the old woman. *I Puri Daj* put an arm around Mary. It felt so comforting that Mary told Sofia's grandmother about Elizabeth and the baby, about Papa and about dwindling coins. She even told of her worries about Jake. *I Puri Daj* and Sofia were still—only making murmuring sounds to let Mary know they were listening.

When Mary finished, all the old woman said was, "So, ve haf a lot to think about, Mary Bunyan, no?"

"*I Puri Daj* always comes up with the answers, Mary." Sofia's voice was filled with confidence.

"I know that I cannot do anything about my father. Elizabeth is going to go to the *assizes* and do everything she can to get the magistrates to free him, but Papa says that is in God's hands." Mary sighed. "'Tis not so easy for me to accept."

"It is not easy for your Papa to accept, either, Mary Bunyan. It is his faith that makes him accept." *I Puri Daj* marked the last words with emphatic thumps of her finger on the back of Mary's hand.

"What is faith?" Sofia asked.

"Mary Bunyan knows about faith," said *I Puri Daj*.

"I don't," said Mary. "My father is the one with faith in God."

"Vhat about vhen you call for your sister? Do you haf faith that she vill come?"

"Yes, but she has always come. It doesn't take faith."

"Your father feels the same vay about God. John Bunyan has learned that God is alvays faithful. I vatch this John Bunyan. I know."

"So, *Daj*," a man's voice, filled with teasing laughter, startled Mary. "If you have watched Mary's father and you know about faith, are you telling me that you have put your faith in John Bunyan's God?"

"Uncle Timoz!" Sofia jumped up and left Mary's side.

"Timoz," *I Puri Daj* said with mock disgust, "is a bad son who should not listen to vomen's conversations."

"The boys have found your brother." He put his hand on Mary's shoulder. "I did not think you would mind if he stayed for a time with the bear. They will bring him to us later."

"Thank you, sir." Mary felt relieved. "Was he with . . . anyone when you found him?"

"No. He wanders the fair, following the dancing bear."

Mary wondered about that loose shoe leather she had heard behind Gifre. Was she wrong? Had Jake been with Gifre and left? She decided not to even voice her fears to Jake.

"Uncle Timoz, is it a shame to be Christ-killers?" Sofia blurted the question. Mary could tell it had been bothering her ever since Gifre hurled the ugly curse at her.

"Vhere did you hear that, *Chey?*" her grandmother asked softly.

"The boy who used his peashooter to shoot gravel at Mary, he said *Rom* are Christ-killers." Her voice was sad. "It is not the first time someone has said this to me."

"Why would he say that, sir?" Mary was puzzled. "Christ was crucified hundreds of years ago by the Romans at the urging of religious leaders of the day. My father says so."

"You are right, Mary, but superstition has long held my people responsible." Timoz sighed.

"Is it true?" Sofia asked.

"Yes and no." Timoz pulled something up to their circle and sat down. Sofia moved over next to him. "Tell them the legend, *Daj.*"

"Alvays haf our people been tinkers," she began, "for as long as ve can remember stories. Vhen *Yeshua ben Miriam—*"

"That means Jesus, Son of Mary," interrupted Timoz.

"Yes, yes. Vhen Jesus was alive, the *Rom* heard about Him and about the miracles He performed. They traveled in their caravans to be near, so that they could see Him and hear vhat He said, alvays trying to keep out of sight."

"Why did they keep out of sight?" asked Mary.

"Our people have always been outcasts," Sofia said matter-of-factly.

"The story is told," Timoz continued, "that when the decision was made to crucify *Yeshua*—your Jesus—the Roman soldiers bought the nails from a Gypsy tinker."

"Oh, Uncle Timoz, no!" Sofia had obviously never heard this story before.

"Sofia, it is just legend. Neighbor Bunyan says that it is not in God's book," Timoz reassured her.

"That is right." Mary thought this was an evil story. "My father read to us from the Bible every night and I have never heard this story."

"Sometimes legends continue because they give people a reason for their hatred," Timoz said sadly.

"But when I asked you if we were Christ-killers, you said 'yes and no.'" Sofia was puzzled.

"As soon as *I Puri Daj* brings us some food," Timoz said, "we will eat and I will tell you why I answered yes."

Sofia's grandmother got up to get them a meal. The smell of bread had been making Mary's stomach rumble. It must be time for the midday meal. She must soon come up with some kind of plan, for she needed to collect Jake and get home in time to take food to Papa. She was no closer to a plan than she was at the beginning of the day.

*I Puri Daj* returned and placed a hot, flat cake of bread in Mary's lap. It was wrapped in a piece of cheesecloth so it wouldn't burn Mary's hands. Sofia hummed as she helped her *baba* serve the meal.

"Here." Sofia tapped Mary on the ankle. "Right beside your foot is your cider."

"Thank you." From the sounds and smells, Mary knew the others had begun to eat, so she bit into her loaf. "Umm, this is good," she said as soon as her mouth was clear. It had a sweet meaty filling.

"I haf one for your brother, too. He vill be hungry vhen he returns."

Mary was overcome with their kindness. "I am so lucky that Sofia found me today. You have been so kind."

"Not luck, Mary," said Timoz. "Your father prays for you. He is my friend, and I am happy to help his family."

"Oh, do not say *help* to Mary." Sofia laughed and poked Mary in the ribs. "Mary doesn't like to take help."

Mary had to smile when Sophia teased. Just hearing her laughter made Mary's independence seem a little foolish.

*I Puri Daj* came to Mary's defense. "Mary Bunyan vorks hard to be able to do things on her own. I, too, vould not vant to take vhat some people call help."

"Uncle Timoz, will you tell us why you said we are Christ-killers?" Sofia was still worried. Mary could hear it in her voice.

"Sofia, I do not mean that the *Rom* are responsible for killing *Yeshua*." Timoz paused. "We, including Mary, are responsible in a way."

"Me?" Mary was surprised.

Timoz reached inside his vest and pulled something out. It was a cross made of four hand-forged intersecting nails. It hung from a leather thong. "When I heard Neighbor Bunyan tell the story of *Yeshua*—"

"My father?" Mary interrupted.

"Yes. I heard him speak. His words were powerful, but even more powerful was the story he told." Timoz continued, "He told of our sin—that burden that weighs us down. He told of Holy God, who cannot bear to look at sin and the gulf that separates sinful man and Holy God."

"Gulf? Vhat is this gulf?" *I Puri Daj* had been listening to Timoz.

"God loves us and wants us to be with Him forever, but we are sinful," he answered. "*Daj*, you know all about *mahrime*."

"Yes." The old woman shifted. "Ve are much afraid of being *mahrime*—unclean. You do not see all the vashing and cleansing I do, Mary Bunyan, to keep this *kumpania* pure. We call it *zuhho*—pure. It is not just clean on the outside; *zuhho* means pure on the inside."

"And are you able to keep us *zuhho?*" Timoz waited for an answer that didn't come. Mary realized this was not a subject that *I Puri Daj* could freely discuss in front of *gadje*.

"No matter how hard you work, *Daj*, we still fight *mahrime*," said Timoz. "Our people have found that it is not possible to be *zuhho*. Mary's father calls *mahrime* sinfulness."

"So, you say that God is *zuhho* and ve are *mahrime?*"

"Yes, *Daj*," Timoz said. "That is the problem."

"Hmmm. I understand this gulf you talk about." *I Puri Daj* sounded sad. "*A zuhho* God can never touch *mahrime* man."

"So does God do like *Rom* and stay far away from anything *mahrime?*" Sofia asked.

"No, that's the wonderful part," Timoz said. "God loves us even though we are sinful—*mahrime*."

Mary listened carefully. She had heard her father talk about sin many times, but she had never heard it told like this. "My father says a price must be paid for our sin."

"A price? You mean unless we pay, we can never be with God?" Sofia didn't understand. "What is the price we must pay?"

"The price for sin is death." Timoz spoke softly, but Mary could hear the intake of Sofia's breath as she gasped.

"What does this have to do with killing Christ?" asked Sofia.

"Everything," Timoz answered. "Because we cannot be good enough on our own, God had to make a way for us to become sinless—to make us *ʒuhho*."

"If we work very hard, can we not become sinless?" Mary was determined to try.

"No, Mary," said Timoz. "Only one sinless man was ever born on this earth and that was *Yeshua*."

"How do you know this, Timoz?" asked *I Puri Daj*, the skepticism plain in her voice.

"The story is told in the Holy Book—the Bible—that Neighbor Bunyan reads to us," Timoz continued. "God wants us to be with Him forever, so He sent His Son, His perfect, *ʒuhho* Son, to become a man and, even worse, to die instead of us."

"You mean He died *for us?*" Sofia sounded confused.

"Yes, Sofia. It was our sin that caused His death, not these nails."

"My sin caused Him to die." Sofia's voice paused, as if turning this information over and looking at it from all sides. "I never knew that."

Timoz handed the cross to Mary. It was heavy in her hand. Was this the reason that her father was willing to go to prison for his faith? It was confusing.

"Uncle Timoz, you sound like a follower of John Bunyan. How can that be? You are *Rom*." Sofia sounded more confused than Mary.

"Oh, no, Sofia." Timoz laughed. "I'm not a follower of John Bunyan. He is my friend and my brother. I am a follower of *Yeshua ben Miriam*—of Jesus Christ."

Mary handed the cross back to Timoz.

"This cross I keep to remind me of the burden of sin that was lifted by *Yeshua's* sacrifice," he said.

After a long pause, *I Puri Daj* sighed deeply. "Vell," she said thoughtfully, "this is something new for our people. I vill haf to think about this, Timoz."

She turned toward Mary and took both of Mary's hands into hers. "Tell me vhat plans you haf hatched this morning, little chicken. Vhat vill put coins in the pocket of Mary Bunyan?"

"*I Puri Daj*, I have not thought of a single thing!" Tears began to sting Mary's eyes. She had made a new friend, listened to stories, eaten her fill, enjoyed the gentle love of a grandmother . . . and completely forgotten her mission. How could she have been so careless?

"Mary Bunyan," *I Puri Daj* squeezed her hands, "just tell me vhat you saw today."

Mary told her about the doves and the animals, about the tradesmen and the fishmongers, about the sounds and smells. *Tinkling, tinkling. Why does a tinkling sound keep coming to my mind?*

"I almost forgot to tell you the funniest sight of all!" Mary described the couple she and Jake had seen.

"Hmmm," said *I Puri Daj*. "Tell me again about his clothes."

Mary described everything she could remember, right down to the tinkling sound.

"That tinkling sound . . ." The old woman sounded thoughtful. "Ve need to think about that sound."

"The tinkling sound?" Mary didn't see any answer at first, but something was beginning to stir. *Could it work? But it is so complicated. If I can—*

The old woman clapped her hands, as if to applaud Mary. "Ve vill see, Mary Bunyan, vhat plan you make."

Mary realized that *I Puri Daj* understood. The seed of a plan had just been germinated. Now to see if it would grow.

"I must get to work." Mary jumped off the stool, just as she heard the slap of Jake's loose sole.

"I'm back," said that familiar voice. "Did you have fun, Mary?" He didn't even stop to get an answer. "I saw the bear dance, an' I got to feed him a honeycomb, an' then—"

"Jake, you little beast!"

"Aw, Mary, I'm sorry."

"He is back and no harm done," Timoz whispered in Mary's ear.

Timoz was right. Besides, she had much to accomplish and she would need Jake's help.

"Thank you, Sofia. Thank you, Timoz. Thank you, *I Puri Daj.* I am so glad I have found friends." Mary felt a faint tingle of hope. Now, if she could just make the plan work somehow.

"Come, Jake. Let's go home. We have work to do."

# Putting the
# Pieces in Place

"Elizabeth, you are up!" Mary heard her stepmother bustling around the cottage.

"Aye. You didn't expect me to continue to lie abed for weeks?" She teasingly pulled on one of Mary's curls. "Where were you yesterday? I feared we would have to hold the service without you."

"Well . . . there were so many errands to do, it took most of the day." Mary was uncomfortable. She did not want to lie to Elizabeth, but she wasn't ready to let her and Bets in on the plan, either. It was still too early. Why get their hopes up?

"Mary?"

"What?"

"I asked you—what errands?" An edge of impatience was beginning to creep into Elizabeth's voice.

"You know I took Papa's dinner, and before that—"

"Elizabeth, are you going out?" Bets walked into the room. "You look so pretty."

Never had Mary been so grateful for an interruption.

"Aye," answered Elizabeth. "I plan to travel to London sometime after the first of next year."

"To London? But that is three days by coach!" said Bets.

"How well I know." Elizabeth spoke in a bold voice, but Mary heard the uncertainty behind it. "I must see Judge Sir Matthew Hale to obtain a pardon for your father. They say Sir Matthew is sympathetic to *dissenters*. If that does not serve, there will be nothing left but to plead before the *assizes* in Bedford."

"Oh, Elizabeth." It sounded overwhelming to Mary.

"Today, I will meet again with the Clerk of Peace, Paul Cobb, to see how I can arrange all this."

"Are you well enough to go?" asked Bets.

"I think so. Anyway, there is no help for it. I will not see your father stay in prison one day longer than he must," answered Elizabeth.

Guilt weighed on Mary for deceiving Elizabeth, but Mary was more determined than ever to work out the plan. Not only did they need money for food and to pay taxes on the cottage, but they also had Papa's keep in jail. And now they would need money for Elizabeth to travel! *I cannot lose any time putting this plan together.*

Elizabeth hurriedly gave instructions to the sisters. They were to care for baby Thomas, watch Jake, sweep the floors, air out the cottage, fix the meal, and take dinner to Papa.

"Give John my love." Elizabeth was still giving orders as she walked out the door. "Tell him I will visit him tomorrow and that I am well."

"We will, Elizabeth." Mary shut the door behind her, letting out her pent-up breath.

"There is much to be done," Bets said.

"I cannot help you today." Mary knew she had no time to argue with Bets.

"What do you mean?" Bets sounded puzzled. "You heard Elizabeth give us instructions."

"I know, but I must work on the plan." Mary paused. "I'm taking Jake with me."

"I see," Bets said. "Tell me what you worked out and how I can help."

"You can help by doing both of our tasks here at home."

"I will be happy to do that. Now . . . tell me the plan."

"Not yet, Bets," said Mary. "I want to settle the particulars first."

"Mary!" said Bets in an exasperated tone. "Tell me! I hate it when you keep secrets."

"I cannot bear to raise your hopes until I have all the parts in place. I am not trying to be secretive."

"Oh, yes, you are—you are hiding everything from me." Bets's voice rose. "You make me ever so angry, Mary." Her voice moved away. "Keep your blasted plan to yourself. Keep your worries to yourself. Why, you can even keep your self to yourself!"

"I will return in time to take Papa's soup." Mary suppressed a sigh. There was no time to argue.

⚜    ⚜    ⚜    ⚜

"Where we going, Mary? Back to see the dancing bear?" Jake buzzed with energy.

"No, the tannery." Mary was still unhappy about her fight with Bets.

"The tannery?"

"Aye. 'Tis over on Queenshead Lane, next to the *lime* kilns."

"Why are we going there?" Jake was puzzled.

"Jake, will you stop asking questions and take me there?"

"Awright." Jake's voice betrayed his disappointment.

The journey along Mill Lane was becoming familiar to Mary. They turned up High Road, passed Bedford *Gaol* on their way toward St. Peters, then turned left at Queenshead Lane. Mary smelled the rancid odor of the tannery on the right side of the road. Luckily, the tanning pits were well off the road—no danger of stumbling in.

Jake led her to the door and Mary knocked. When the door creaked open, Mary asked to speak to the tanner. She told Jake to wait outside while she went in.

She was not gone overly long. When she came out, a long bag that looked like a mattress ticking without the straw dragged behind.

"What is that, Mary?" Jake asked.

"'Tis a bag for collecting *pure*. This is going to be your job, Jake. You are to collect *pure*."

"*Pure?* What is *pure?*"

"*Pure* is another word for dung," Mary answered.

"Dung?" Jake sounded like an echo.

"You know what dung is, Jake."

"Oh, no, Mary!" Jake backed away. "I will not touch that stuff."

"'Tis dry." Mary was getting exasperated. "'Twill not hurt you one bit, Master John Bunyan, the Younger."

"Mary!" Jake was desperate.

"Do you know that we are almost broke?"

"Broke?"

"Aye. Broke. We are nearly out of money. No money for food, no money for Papa's bill at jail, no money for anything!" Mary was tired of having to fight her whole family. "Papa asked me to take care of everyone—"

"Elizabeth takes care of the family." Jake's voice held a stubborn tone.

"I know, but—"

"You are just being bossy, Mary."

"Jake!" Mary's throat tightened. "Jake, I cannot do this by myself. I need your help."

"You need my help?" echoed Jake, the stubbornness fading from his voice. He was quiet for a time. "Awright, Mary. I will help." He took the bag and they started out.

"The tanner said that hen, pigeon, and goose turds are the best, but dog dung will work as well," Mary said. They worked their way down along the banks of the Ouse, under the Swan Bridge, where goose *pure* was abundant.

"'Tis foul. It smells loathsome and sticks to my hands. You said 'twas dry. I cannot believe I have a full sack of manure," Jake said. "What are you planning to do with this?"

"I will not do anything with it." Mary laughed. "We take it to the tanner. They make an infusion of *pure* and water for *baiting* of the hides."

"Huh? *Baiting?*"

"To make leather, the tanner first *limes* the hides. That takes many days. After the hides are properly *limed,* they are laid in a *baiting dub,* to open the pores. *Baiting* is made of dung and water."

"Pee-yuu!"

"I know," Mary said. "'Tis why it smells putrid around the tannery. After the skins are *baited,* they are put in the *oozing* —powdered oak bark that fills the open pores and preserves the skins. Finally, the skins are tanned and *curried.*"

"So the tanner will pay us for the *pure?*" Jake asked.

"No, 'tis not that easy. Have patience, Jake. When all the pieces are in place, I shall tell you."

They dragged the bag back to the tannery. Jake brought it around back while the tanner gave Mary a bag filled with strips of leather. Mary promised to hunt *pure* for him again next week.

As they walked down High Road, Mary told Jake that she must stop at the lacemaker's cottage. With Jake smelling like the *baiting dub,* Mary left him to wait near the Crown Pub and made her way alone to the lacemaker. Shortly, she came out with another parcel. Jake caught up with her.

"What ya got, Mary?" he asked.

"You are full of questions today, brother."

"So you will not tell me?"

"Aye. We have one more stop." Mary knew this would please him. "Would you like to visit the dancing bear?"

"Oh, Mary! Can we?"

"First stop—the river, so you can clean up," Mary said, crushing a sprig of rosemary between her fingers.

"So, ve haf put our plan into action," *I Puri Daj* said, her arm warm and welcoming around Mary.

"Aye. I have one favor to ask Timoz." Mary was glad to find Timoz at the encampment.

"Anything for the daughter of Neighbor Bunyan," Timoz said.

"This is not charity, Timoz. 'Tis a business proposition." Mary wanted to be clear.

Sofia laughed. "So soon you forget, Uncle Timoz? Mary does not like to take help." The girl poked Mary in the ribs, teasing her once again.

"What is this business proposition?"

Mary outlined the plan. *I Puri Daj* made soft, encouraging noises while she talked. When she finished, Timoz spoke.

"A good plan and happy I will be to work for you. Your father will be proud of you, Mary. I will come to your cottage before the *kumpania* leaves on *O Longo Drom*."

"Thank you, Timoz," Mary replied, grateful for his help. Now she only had one piece of the puzzle to put into place, but not till tomorrow.

"Mary, come with me," Sofia whispered. "I want to show you something."

"What, Sofia?" Mary was curious. Her new friend seemed excited.

Sofia put something in Mary's hand.

"Why, 'tis Timoz's cross. How do you come to have it?" asked Mary.

"After we talked yesterday, I could not stop thinking about *Yeshua* and being *mahrime*—sinful. I asked Timoz if *Yeshua*—Jesus Christ—would take my burden of sin away and make me *ʒuhho*. Do you know what Timoz said?" Sofia talked in a whispery voice.

"What?" Mary was intrigued.

"Because I knew I was sinful—*mahrime*—and wanted to become pure, and because I knew that the only way to become pure was through the death of Jesus Christ, Timoz said that I was a believer too." Sofia sounded happy.

"Just like that?" Mary asked.

"Yes. Timoz helped me pray."

"What did you pray?"

"I told God I knew I couldn't become *ʒuhho* on my own, that I need *Yeshua*—Christ. Without Him, I would remain *mahrime* forever, no matter how hard I tried. I thanked God for sending His Son. I thanked Jesus Christ for dying and paying for my sin so that I wouldn't die. I thanked Him for accepting me—me, Mary, nothing but a *Rom chey*—into the family of God."

"Oh, Sofia." Mary stretched out her hand to touch Sofia's face and felt tears. "Does this make you sad?"

"No, Mary. It makes me full. My heart cannot hold it all." Sofia reached up and took Mary's hand. "Timoz gave me his cross of nails to help me remember to depend on this One who died for me."

"I am glad that you found this happiness, Sofia," Mary said.

※     ※     ※     ※

Mary and Jake walked more slowly on the way home. The bags from the tanner and the lacemaker were tucked safely under Jake's arms. Mary had much to think about. Nearly all the pieces of the plan were in place. Tomorrow would tell.

And Sofia . . . No one had ever shared secrets with her besides Bets. Sofia confided that she had prayed to see Mary today and tell her about Timoz's cross. Sofia's trust cemented their friendship. Mary was happy that Sofia had decided to put her faith in God. For herself, though, she disliked the idea of dependence, even on God.

"I-can-do-all-things . . . I-can-do-all-things," Mary repeated softly.

"What?" asked Jake.

"Oh, nothing. I'm just happy about our work today."

## 9

# Uproar
## at the Cottage

S hould I believe the talk I heard about you and Jake traips-
ing all over Bedford—including the gypsy encampment
over by the fair?" Elizabeth asked with a no-nonsense tone.

Mary hated it when Elizabeth tried to sound like a mother.
She absently fingered the length of soft silk ribbon in her
apron pocket.

"Mary?"

"We were out doing errands." Mary would not back
down. She disliked arguing with Elizabeth, but Mary had
done nothing wrong. Were it not for her plan, this family
would soon be scrounging to stock the soup pot.

"Errands? I gave you girls instructions before I left yesterday. They did not include errands, did they?" asked Elizabeth. "And you left Bets with all the work?"

"Aye. I feel badly about that part, but I am struggling to
take care of this family." Mary was exasperated. "There was
work to do."

"Why do you presume you must take care of the family?" Elizabeth was puzzled.

"When Papa was arrested, he charged me to care for all of you."

"Oh, Mary," said Elizabeth sadly, "your father meant for you to help me, not exclude me."

"We are nearly penniless! How do we buy food or pay Papa's—?"

"Do you think I am unaware of these things, Mary?" Elizabeth said. "During the time I lay abed, I asked God to intercede for us. I meet with some of the elders of your father's church tomorrow."

"No, Elizabeth!" Mary said. "The Bunyans must not be reduced to begging." She paced. "I came up with a plan to replenish our funds. Yesterday I began putting the pieces in place."

"Why did you not tell me this, Mary?" Elizabeth took Mary's arm to stop her pacing. Elizabeth's voice shook. "Why keep everything to yourself?"

"'Tis for our family I am doing this, yet everyone is mad at—"

"Mary Bunyan!" Bets shouted from the dooryard, but her voice filled the cottage. "Mary, where are you?" Bets was already inside the common room by the time she finished her question, so Mary saw no need to answer.

"Bets, what is the matter?" Elizabeth asked. "Calm down, take a deep breath, and tell me what is wrong."

"Mary, do you not want to tell Elizabeth what is wrong?" Bets asked.

"Bets, Thomas is asleep," Elizabeth reminded her.

"I am sorry." Bets took a deep breath. "I am humiliated. Mary took Jake all over the town yesterday—in the good parts, in the bad parts, by all of our friends' houses, down by the river." A pause. "Do you know what they were doing, Elizabeth?"

"Bets," Mary said, "why don't you get on with the telling, since you are enjoying it so much."

"Aye, then. They were collecting dung. I was told that they were not particular—chicken dung, goose turds, dog manure—"

"What!" Elizabeth's voice rose an octave.

"Yes, Elizabeth, you heard true. My sister and my brother were picking up dung all over town." Bets wasn't through. "And you know who made sure I knew this? Gifre. He's spreading the word to anyone who will listen."

Mary could say nothing. *Gifre. Could things get any worse?*

"Is this true, Mary?" Elizabeth asked.

"'Tis not as bad as it sounds." Mary tried to convince herself.

"So . . . 'tis true."

"Well, yes. But 'tis part of the plan I worked out. When all the pieces are in place—"

"Mary," said Elizabeth, "I must hear this plan now."

"I cannot tell you till I speak to Father." Mary knew that Elizabeth and Bets were angry. "When I put the final piece in place, 'twill become clear."

Mary sensed an air of frustration in that room as tangibly as if it had dimension. Since nothing more could be said, she turned and made her way out of the cottage. *When they see the whole plan, they will understand. Well . . . Papa will understand, anyway.* At least someone would be proud of her accomplishments. *Why did Papa have to go to jail?*

She opened the door of Papa's workshop. At the workbench she gingerly ran her hands around the edge, careful of slivers. She felt each hook until she came to one with a scrap bag on it. The bag was only half full. She felt the rest of the hooks. Nothing.

Getting on her hands and knees, she carefully ran her fingers over the sawdust floor, collecting each scrap of sheet metal she could find. She tried to work methodically, to miss nothing. The warmth of the forge was long gone and the room was as chilled as Mary's spirits.

"Ouch!" She sat back and probed her knee with her fingers until she found the sliver of metal. It gave her shivers to pull it out. Did it tear her stocking? Not a very big hole. Good. She was thankful for that. Her fingers felt the stickiness of blood. She smiled to herself. *At least that will keep the hole from tearing farther until I can ask Bets to mend it.*

Bets. How to mend her relationship with Bets was a bigger puzzle. She loved her sister. Bets was more than a sister, she was a friend and, a good part of the time, she was Mary's eyes. *I'm sorry Bets. 'Twill be made up to you. You shall see.*

And Elizabeth. Since Papa's arrest, Mary had come to appreciate her for the first time. *Did I ruin everything? Should I have told her the plan?* There was no time to dwell on it. She needed to take these things to Papa.

Last night Jake had laid out the tools Papa would need. Mary wrapped them in a cloth and tucked them inside the bag of scraps, tying strong twine around the opening. She set it on the bench next to yesterday's two bags. *Where is Jake? I need his help taking this to Papa.* Lately, every time she needed Jake, he was gone. He'd worked hard yesterday—she had to give him that.

She knotted all three bags together so they could be slung over her shoulder, leaving a free hand for Papa's soup. How to manage to get to Papa with all this?

"I-can-do-all-things . . . I-can-do-all-things . . ."

*Almost there. Only about half a furlong to go,* thought Mary. *No, I'm going to have to put these down and rest for a time.* She leaned over to the left and let the sacks slide off her shoulder onto the road—making sure she didn't spill the soup in the crock. *Ahhhhh.* It felt good to be rid of that heavy burden.

As she set the crock down to hoist the bags back onto her shoulder, her hand brushed what felt like a rope on the ground. No, it was two pieces of rope, one on either side of her . . . or had it been a rope that had stretched across the road. Gifre? Could it have been Gifre trying to trip her? She remembered the pebbles that had been scattered across the path just a few days ago.

But someone had cut this booby trap, saving her a terrible fall. Could Timoz be looking out for her? Sofia?

She hefted the bags back up, carefully picked up the jug of soup, and continued on her way. Was that the flap of a loose sole in the distance? She chided herself for a vivid imagination.

"Mary! How did you ever make it all the way over here with the weight of those sacks?" Her father's voice was incredulous. "Where is your brother?"

"I wanted to bring this to you, Papa, and see what you thought before I told everyone."

"I see," Papa said thoughtfully. "You are trying to save the world all by yourself again."

"Oh, Papa." Mary could recognize his teasing voice. "Just remember, you must not ever call me 'wee' Mary again."

Papa laughed. He was kneading her shoulders with his big hands. It felt good. She knew Papa would be proud.

"You had best eat your soup before it gets any colder." Mary pulled the cloth and spoon out of her apron pocket.

"Show me your wares as I eat, my good missus," Papa said.

"'Tis best to start at the beginning. You know we are very nearly out of food and money, do you not?" Mary asked.

"Elizabeth and I have spoken of this. She meets with the congregation tomorrow. And Paul Cobb obtained permission for prisoners to perform some kind of labor in prison to help pay our keep and support our families." He took another slurp of soup. "'Tis not for you to worry, little one. God will care for us."

"Oh, Papa. I not only worried, but I have a perfect plan. Jake and I visited the St. Andrew's Day Fair and saw a man in fancy dress. He had hundreds of ribbons on him—some looped on his breeches for decoration, some lacing up slits and jags sliced through his garments, and others lacing his vest and breeches closed."

"Ah, Mary, I can picture the peacock you describe. Jake exaggerated not one whit."

"Each lace, the fancy ones as well as the plain leather laces, had a metal tip."

"That's right. They are called tagged laces," said her father. "What has this to do with your plan?"

Mary untied the twine on the tanner's sack. "Look, Father. Leather strips."

"Where did you get such fine leather, Mary? And how, with no coin?"

"I had to devise a way to provide the tanner with something he needed in exchange for the leather. I discovered he needs *pure* for *baiting* the leather." Mary paused as her father burst into laughter.

"Don't tell me, Mary—you collected *pure!*"

"Not exactly. Jake did it for me."

"Bless his heart."

"But I arranged it with the tanner, Papa. I thought of it all by myself." Mary was proud of her resourcefulness.

"Hmm. I would be careful of how you tell Elizabeth." He laughed again and said under his voice, "I would dearly love to see her face . . ."

"Regrettably, 'tis too late for that, Papa. She knows and is none too pleased." Mary, changing the subject, reached for the next bag. "Here are ribbons and laces."

"However did you manage these, Mary? They must have cost a king's ransom."

"These are not first quality. They are seconds—the short ribbon ends and lace pieces that have a thickened warp thread. They will make perfect tagged laces. I offered Bets's services to warp Goodwife Emory's ribbon looms each morning in exchange for her seconds."

"Mary, you amaze me."

"The other bag is your scrap bag. I think there are metal pieces enough to tag all of these laces. Jake helped me gather some of your tools." Mary asked the last question, "Will you be allowed to make tagged laces here in jail?" Everything hinged on this answer.

"Aye. I even have a small bench near my mat."

"You know Timoz, the *Rom* believer?"

"Aye. You have met my friend Timoz?"

"Timoz and his family are my friends too. Timoz will buy the laces from us. He will peddle them along with his other wares as they travel."

Mary felt Papa's big arms surround her. 'Twas an embrace she sorely needed.

"Mary, will you pray with me? I am filled with gratitude—I wish to speak to our heavenly Father."

"Aye."

"Father." Papa paused, as if to think of everything that word implied. "Beloved Father, I come to You with this cherished daughter You gave me. Thank You for her. She is more precious to me than all I own."

Mary snuggled deeper into her father's approval.

"Thank You for Elizabeth and her steadfast love. Even now she is caring for my family while I am serving You in prison."

*Elizabeth? Caring for the family?* Mary stiffened. *I am the one—*

"And I offer thanks for Bets . . . for the soup she lovingly prepares each day. And now for her willingness to take on the job with the looms."

*Willingness? She doesn't even know.*

"I thank You for my son Jake, who is watching out for his sisters."

*Watching out?* Mary sniffed. *If Papa knew how out-of-control his precious Jake was!*

". . . and for his readiness to perform a distasteful task— he is learning servanthood. Keep little Thomas safe and well. Bless all of our friends who have come to our aid in this time of need—Neighbor Winswode, the tanner; Goodwife Emory . . ."

*He's thanking God for the tanner and the lacemaker? Papa, this was me. Me! I did this by myself.*

"Thank You for my friend Timoz, who will buy these laces. Most of all, Lord, I thank You for Your provision. You have demonstrated that I can depend upon Your promise to care for my family. Amen."

Mary did not trust herself to speak.

"Is there something wrong, Mary?" Papa was puzzled.

"I labored for days to make this plan work, Papa." Mary moved out of his embrace, putting distance between them. "I did it all by myself. I depended on no one. Yet you have given credit to Elizabeth, to Bets, to Jake . . . why, even to the lace-maker and the tanner." Mary shook her head as if to clear the jumbled thoughts. "I know God provides for us, Papa, but it took much toil on my part to help Him with His provision."

"Oh, my wee Mary. We are back to that, are we? I am proud of you. This is a wonderful plan. It will put food on our table for a long time to come." He sighed. "I take nothing away from you—'tis brilliant. But 'twill take the work of our whole family to accomplish it."

He pulled her back next to him, unwilling to let a gulf come between them. "Had you shared your ideas with the family, 'twould have eased their worry." He waited for a response, but when none came, he continued. "By trying to do this on your own, you've robbed yourself of the joy that comes with working together." He paused. "You've heard the old saying, 'All is well that ends well'? I cannot agree. 'Tis not the final destination that God cares most about—but the journey itself."

"I do not understand." Mary was puzzled.

"Which do you think is more pleasing to God: when we stop along life's way to encourage fellow pilgrims on the journey, or when we step over struggling pilgrims and race to a spectacular finish?"

Mary didn't answer. "I'd better be heading back to the cottage, Papa."

Papa helped her knot the soup crock and the spoon into the cloth. "Think about this, Mary, my dearest one—I love you and God loves you. You are strong and you are brave, but you cannot do it all in your own strength."

Mary started back, tired, discouraged, and confused. *I tried my hardest and everyone is mad at me.* Without thinking, she mouthed the words that always seemed to help, "I-can-do-all-things . . . I-can-do-all-things . . ." But this time the tears started to flow.

*Who am I fooling?* she thought. *I can't do anything right!*

# 10
# Gifre's
# Attack

As Mary moved away from the jail, the tears that threatened to spill could be held back no longer. Her eyes brimmed with moisture. She pressed on the lower lids trying to stem the tide, but it would not be stanched. As the tears coursed down her face, her nose joined the torrent. With the knotted bundle swinging from one arm, she couldn't swipe her face fast enough. She must look a sniveling mess. How could she go back to the cottage like this? Slow, deep breaths helped as she struggled for control.

Thankfully, Mill Lane seemed uncommonly quiet for mid-afternoon. Because her hands had been filled with the three bags and the soup she carried to Papa, she had not brought her cane. Without it to negotiate the road ahead, she depended on her sensitive feet. She always wore shoes made of supple leather—both uppers and sole—the more worn, the better. With her cane she would have gained speed, but the way home was so familiar, her feet practically knew every cobble.

Goodwife Harbin's geese honked at her. Fortunately, a picket fence stood between them—a guard dog was less of a threat than a goose protecting his property. Mary knew that the whack of an irate gander's head could topple someone much bigger than she.

Somewhere off to her left, someone was tunelessly humming. *Will I ever have anything to hum about?* she wondered. She caught the scrape of scampering feet ahead to her right, very near the Dissenting Meetinghouse. A child playing. *And will I ever play again?* Her shoulders ached from the weight of the sacks she had earlier carried to Papa. It seemed like hours had passed since she had made her way to the jail.

*Stop it! Stop feeling sorry for yourself.* She swiped the last of the tears off her cheeks with the back of her hand and straightened her shoulders. Hoisting the cloth with the mug and spoon, she hurried her pace. *Just remember—the plan worked. It worked.*

The scurrying sounds ceased, but she breathed the dust raised by the movement. Mary suspected that the person she heard moving stopped to watch her go by. How she hated the feeling of being watched. "Hello? Are you playing?" Nothing. She quickened her step again, but something felt wrong.

She crossed in front of the meetinghouse, as she always did. Why was the old beech tree rustling like that? She stopped. Except for a few stubborn leaves, the branches must be bare. Strange.

Why did her mind go to Gifre? His house was very close to the back of the property, but—

Thwack! A branch lashed across her face with walloping force, slamming her to the ground backward. She could hardly get her breath. Her cheek felt like it was broken. *What happened?* Was that Gifre . . . laughing . . . running in the opposite direction?

*No! Please, no.* Mary heard Jake—her own brother—running away. The flap of that loose sole was unmistakable. *Calm down, Mary. First things first. Get up. Get up.* She summoned every bit of courage she could muster.

She used her arms to push herself up on her elbows, but a stabbing pain took her breath away. Her leg was injured. Until someone came along to help, she was stuck.

What happened? Mary's fingers probed the bones of her face. The damaged side was swelling. She spat out blood that filled her mouth. *I refuse to dwell on Jake . . .*

The pain made her queasy. *I can wait until help comes. I know I can. What does it matter that everyone is angry with me?* Mary was having a hard time keeping up her brave disguise.

"I-can-do-all-things . . . I-can-do-all-things," she said aloud, as if speaking would make it so. *Stop fooling yourself, Mary,* she chided herself. *There is no doubt that Jake partnered with Gifre in this attack. Papa is disappointed in me. I've let Elizabeth down. Bets is mad at me for shutting her out. Now I cannot get up because something is wrong with my leg, my head hurts, my face is injured beyond recognition, and . . . I'm blind.* "I can't do anything!" Mary screamed the words that ended in a flood of tears, but no one witnessed her descent into Papa's Slough of Despond.

For the second time that day, Mary wept. As she managed to pull herself to a sitting position, she discovered that Papa's mug was shattered. Shattered! How was she ever to replace it? The tears turned to sobs until she was hiccoughing with despair. She had no concept of time, but eventually her crying eased.

A sense of calm followed the weeping. It seemed as if she slept and then woke. Some idea flickered 'round the back of her mind. *Fix your thoughts,* Mary. She couldn't grasp it. It had to do with . . . the missing part. *What missing part?* she wondered. Her verse—she always left off the last phrase. What was it? *Through Christ. Yes. That is it! I can do all things through Christ which strengtheneth me.*

"I can do all things—through Christ which strengtheneth me." Mary said the words as if she were hearing them for the first time. "Through Christ," she repeated, slowly shaking her swollen head.

*How stubborn I have been.* The realization was like a door opening for her. *'Tis like Papa said, I do not have to do it in my strength alone!* Even Sofia chided her about not accepting help.

Mary turned expressive fingers up to heaven, as if to relinquish her control. "Father," she prayed aloud, "forgive me for not doing all things through You. I have been so stubborn and made a mess of everything. Elizabeth and Bets are mad at me. I provoked Jake until he turned on his own family. I pushed away the help of our good neighbors. In missing Mother, I have been cold to Elizabeth."

The pain in Mary's leg was sharp enough to pull her from prayer. Her face throbbed, but she felt calm and lighter—as if a burden had been lifted from her shoulders. Almost like when Papa removed her heavy sacks. *Oh, Father, how have I lived without You?* This time she was not thinking of Papa.

Before she had time to ponder this question, she heard the

sound of Jake running toward her, followed by the voice of Elizabeth. "Mary, are you hurt?"

Just before Mary slid off into unconsciousness, she thought, *My brother . . . Jake . . . brought help. Thank You, Father.*

# The Healing Begins

Mary groaned as she woke. "Where am I?"

"Elizabeth. Mary is awake!" Bets must have been sitting beside the bed. "You are in bed in the downstairs alcove. How do you feel?"

"Battered."

"I'm so glad you are back with us, Mary." It was Elizabeth. "By the time I reached you, you were unconscious."

"How did you get me home?"

"I sent Jake after your father's handcart. We lifted you as carefully as we were able and then trundled you home."

"So, I was carted home like so much firewood." Mary tried to laugh at her feeble joke, but it hurt too much.

"The doctor is here," announced Jake.

"Everyone into the kitchen while the doctor takes a look at Mary," said Elizabeth.

"Ummm." Mary tried to shake her head to clear the muzziness, but the motion made her dizzy.

"Good. You are awake," said Bets. "As soon as the doctor began poking at your leg, you *swooned* again."

"What did the doctor say?" Mary asked as she heard Elizabeth walk back into the room.

"The bones in your leg are not broken. You must have wrenched it as you fell. Damage has been done to the flesh and *gristle*, but thankfully, nothing permanent." Elizabeth expelled an audible sigh. Many a person in Bedfordshire had died from a broken leg. "You may be concussed from the fall, but only slightly." She pulled at one of Mary's curls. "These springy curls may have come in handy when you hit the back of your head. If the doctor's tale be true, they may have cushioned the blow somewhat."

"Are you teasing, Elizabeth?" Mary could hear the relief in her stepmother's tone of voice.

"Perhaps just a little, wee Mary. I thank God that He spared you any permanent injury." Elizabeth took Mary's hand in her soft fingers and raised it to her lips. "I cannot imagine what we would do without you."

"How can you say that after the way I've treated you?" asked Mary. "As I walked home from visiting Papa, I was filled with shame over the way I treated my family."

"Oh, Mary. If you but knew how we agonized over the things we said to you." Bets sounded very near tears.

"Is Jake here?" asked Mary.

A subdued voice from the corner of the room answered, "Aye."

"Do you have a chair, Jake?"

"No."

"Will you fetch a chair so that you can all be comfortable?" Mary listened. "Is Thomas playing?"

"No," answered Elizabeth. "'Tis evening now. He has already been bedded down."

"Before I say what I am aching to say, what did the doctor say about my face?" Mary's fingers gently probed the swelling around the raised welt that started at her forehead above her right eye had slashed diagonally across her brow, the bridge of her nose, her cheek, and ended on the side of her neck.

Elizabeth answered, "No broken bones there either."

"You shall not want to be asking any of us for a picture of how you look, though," Bets teased.

"Bets!" Elizabeth tried to sound outraged, but Bets's lightheartedness relieved some of the tension of the day. "The doctor said no permanent damage has been done to your face. The blow did not break the skin, so once the swelling goes down, you shall be as comely as ever."

Jake dragged the chair in and sat down. His uneasiness played out in the scuffing of his loose sole on the rung of the chair.

"Before we say another word, I have much to get off my chest. First . . . I must ask forgiveness." Mary was serious now.

"Forgiveness! Mary, what are you talking about?" Elizabeth was puzzled.

"As I walked home from the jail, I was filled with self-pity. I believed I had been toiling to save this family and that no one appreciated me." Mary smiled self-consciously. "Papa exhorted me earlier, in his gentle way, to face the damage my stubbornness caused." Mary paused. "It did not do much to improve my already black mood."

Elizabeth laid a cool cloth across Mary's cheek.

"Thank you." It felt good. Mary continued, "Good thing I did not wallow in the pity overly long. 'Tis not a pretty sight, let me assure you." Mary chuckled when she thought of her eyes and nose running and her shoulders heaving with sobs. "No, 'tis not a pretty sight, but it did not last long. After the pity came some startling revelations."

"Revelations?" asked Jake.

"Aye. Fresh insight into the way I acted toward my family." Mary turned the cloth over to the cooler side. "Papa was right. In my pride, I pushed away the help of both friends and family. I wanted to depend on no one. I was bluffing. 'Twas a sham."

"You don't have to say all this now, Mary," began Elizabeth.

"But I must," insisted Mary. "I spent my life carrying burdens that should have been shared—all because my pride would not allow me to ask for help. Do you know what that did?"

"Did it make you strong?" asked Bets.

"No. It made me push away everyone God sent to help me. Even my friend Sofia chided me about my fear of accepting help." Mary fingered the soft ribbon in her apron pocket while she reached out with her other hand toward her stepmother. "Elizabeth, when you came into our family you seemed to love us from the very start. I feared that if I loved you, I would forget my own mother." Mary connected with

Elizabeth's hand and felt her unspoken encouragement through touch. "How could I have missed welcoming you as a stepmother and a friend?"

"I knew we would eventually be friends, Mary." Elizabeth laid her other hand over Mary's.

"And instead of planning and sharing with you, Bets, I kept everything secret. I am ashamed that you found out about the plan from Gifre." Mary shuddered to think of Gifre. She heard Jake squirming in his chair.

"There is no need to apologize, Mary," said Bets. "We heard about the plan. Elizabeth went to visit Father earlier this evening, to ease his mind, should he have heard about your accident."

"And he *had* heard rumors," added Elizabeth. "He was beside himself with grief and worry. You know how much he loves you."

"I do."

"He was so relieved to hear that you will recover," said Elizabeth.

"But," interrupted Bets, "he told Elizabeth about your plan. He called it 'perfect.' I am sorry for the way I behaved when I heard about the . . . *pure*."

"If I had let the family in on the plan from the beginning, there would have been no shock." Mary laughed a little. "And 'tis not as bad as you have imagined, little sister."

"Believe me, Mary. I shall not question your judgment again." Bets sounded sincere.

"Never again, Bets?" Mary smiled. "Elizabeth, you are my witness."

They all laughed. Somehow nothing seemed as bad when

they teased each other. Mary could hear Jake squirming in his chair again.

"Jake, I need to ask you to forgive me too."

"Me?"

"Aye. I bossed you around and it made you so angry that Gifre was able to turn you against your family." Mary reached out toward Jake, but as she connected with him, she felt him shrink away.

"What d'ya mean, 'turn against'?" Jake sounded prickly.

"'Twas not really your fault, Jake—"

"What are you talking about, Mary?" Jake jumped off his chair and grabbed her arm.

"Ouch!" She was sore all over.

"Jake, sit down," said Elizabeth.

"But, Elizabeth, Mary thinks I did this to her."

"No, Jake, she could not think that." Elizabeth paused. "You cannot think that, can you, Mary?"

"Well . . ." Mary was confused. Had she misheard? "Every time I heard Gifre, I knew that Jake was near."

"How did you know?" asked Jake.

"The sole of your shoe is loose. It makes a distinctive flapping sound," Mary explained.

"So you thought I was helping Gifre," Jake said. "You believe I could do this to you?"

Mary thought about that. "No," she said slowly. In fact, he was the one to bring help this afternoon. "You are right, Jake. You cannot have done this." She remembered his hard work collecting *pure*—how could she have thought it possible?

"Now let me ask forgiveness, Mary," said Jake. "When

Papa was arrested, I was angry that he asked you to take care of Elizabeth and the family. What about me?"

Elizabeth interrupted, "Your father was concerned because I fainted. He did not intend for any of you children to be burdened with caring for this family. Your father and I will always see that you children are cared for."

"I know, Elizabeth," said Jake, "but Mary *was* being bossy about it when you were sick."

"He speaks truth, Elizabeth," admitted Mary. "I did push him around."

"When Gifre started being nice to me," Jake said, "it made me feel important. He asked me to help him spread some dried peas along Mill Lane that day that Mary took soup to Papa. He said it was a treat for the birds. When I saw Mary fall, I knew how bad Gifre was. I was so ashamed I ran."

"So that is why I heard you." Mary had heard correctly.

"Yes. When Timoz found me, the day of the St. Andrew's Day Fair—"

"Whoa! Jake running with Gifre," Elizabeth said. "Mary slipping on peas, the St. Andrew's Day Fair. It sounds like I missed quite a bit of intrigue while I was ill!"

Mary admitted that before they were finished, Elizabeth would undoubtedly hear even more. She promised Elizabeth that from now on, there would be no more secrets.

Jake continued his explanation. While he was making his way back to Mary, on the day of the fair, Timoz told him about Gifre and the peashooter. Jake was horrified to realize that Gifre was determined to torment Mary. He promised Timoz he would watch out for Mary.

"When Bets told me that you had just left to take Papa's

soup, I hurried out to find you," Jake said. "I found that rope stretched across the road to trip you, so I took my knife and cut Gifre's rope in two." He paused. "I was too late to help you the second time. I came just as Gifre let go of one of the rope pieces he rigged, catapulting the branch to hit you."

"I wondered how the branch came to wallop me," said Mary.

"Gifre ran. I knew you needed help, so I ran for Elizabeth first." He was quiet. "I probably should have seen to you first, huh?"

"You need not worry, Brother. I am grateful that you were watching out for me," Mary said. "You have no idea how I worried."

"I didn't want to say I was looking out for you, since you hate to be helped."

Mary laughed. "Not any longer. I shall take all help offered."

"You sound like you've had a real change of heart, Mary," said Bets, putting a fresh cloth on her face.

"That is exactly what I had—a change of heart." Mary was too tired to tell them about her prayer. All she said was, "I learned a new verse—'I can do all things—through Christ which strengtheneth me.'"

Her family quietly left the room as she drifted to sleep.

# 12
## All Things Through Christ

"M ary? Are you awake?" whispered Elizabeth.

"Aye." Mary woke with the sun. She was lying still to keep her leg from aching.

"You have some visitors. Do you feel well enough to see Sofia and her family?"

"Sofia? Here? Oh, yes, Elizabeth. I hoped to see her before she left."

Elizabeth helped scoot Mary up to a sitting position, using quilts to prop her. Mary bit her lip to keep from crying out.

"I'll be in the kitchen heating some of the pear cider that Goodwife Emory brought you as a get-well gift," Elizabeth whispered. "We will serve it to your guests."

Mary heard chairs being pulled into the alcove. Then, before anyone was announced, she was wrapped in a familiar hug.

"*I Puri Daj!* Is it you?" Mary knew it was, from the feel of the grandmotherly embrace and the scent of wood smoke and sweetmeats.

"See for yourself, *Chey*." Mary's hands were placed on the crinkly face.

"No, question," Mary teased, "it is Sofia's *baba*. Did you bring that *Rom chey* with you?" Mary was smiling. She was honored that her friends came. She understood how fearful of *gadje mahrime*—contamination—the *Rom* were. To have them visit the Bunyan cottage was an honor indeed.

"I suppose you mean this *Rom chey*—this Sofia." *O Puri Daj* chuckled.

"Sofia?"

"'Tis I, Mary." Sofia seemed quiet.

"Sofia is surprised by your bumps and bruises, eh, Sofia?" The old woman sat in the creaking chair and Sofia moved close and took Mary's hand.

"Timoz is here too," said Sofia.

"Thank you for coming, Timoz, and bringing *I Puri Daj* and Sofia," said Mary.

"'Tis my pleasure, Mary. When I hear what happened, I want to see you for myself." Timoz was quiet for a time. "You look bad, but no permanent damage. Eh, *Daj?*"

"She vill be fine." *I Puri Daj* patted Mary's hand. "Now I vill go visit your Elizabet. Come, Timoz, Mary Bunyan's brother has been looking like the sheepdog. You must talk to him—tell him you know he vatches Mary Bunyan good. Vas not his fault."

"Sofia? Are you still here?"

"Yes. Does it hurt, Mary?" Sofia sighed deeply. "I wish I had followed you to help you. I am not good friend."

"You are my best friend, Sofia. Best. I do not understand why Gifre did this, but as I lay on the ground, I saw how stubborn I have been." Mary found Sofia's arm and pulled her closer. "I asked God to forgive me for turning my back on those He sent to help me."

"You did?"

"Aye. And I asked Him to forgive me for not putting my trust in Him." Mary shook her head slightly. "All this time when I was struggling with a weight as heavy as your Gypsy caravan—"

Sofia laughed at the image.

"—I cannot believe that the Lord was walking right beside me, ready to carry the burden for me. All I had to do was ask!"

"And did you ask?" Sofia had her teasing voice.

"Yes, my friend, I did. Lying right there on the ground, I let the Lord take my burdens." Mary laughed. "So while I may look pounded and pummeled on the outside, I am healthier than ever on the inside."

Sofia was on the bed hugging Mary.

"Ouch, Sofia," teased Mary. "Don't forget the battered body."

"Sorry, sorry." She scooted back off the bed. "I am happy, Mary. Now we both trust *Yeshua ben Miriam*."

"Mary." Elizabeth had come quietly into the alcove. "Do you feel ready to see Gifre?"

"He's here?" Mary could feel her heart race.

"You do not have to see him. He is here with his father."

"If I wasn't a believer, I'd pound and pummel him," whispered Sofia.

Mary couldn't help herself. She laughed until her cheek felt like it would split. "If I see him, you must promise to say nothing, Sofia." Mary waited for an answer. When none came, she asked again, "Promise?"

"Yes, *Chey*. I will be wondrous kind to the stupid *gadjo*."

Mary doubted not that *Yeshua ben Miriam* still had much work to do on two new believers. If Sofia would try to be 'wondrous kind,' she would agree to see Gifre. "Show them in, Elizabeth."

Sofia chuckled under her breath. "No one trusts these two *gadjo*," she whispered in Mary's ear. "Timoz, Jake, and Elizabeth hover near the doorway, while *I Puri Daj* insists on having a chair pulled close enough to hear. 'Tis a scene worthy of the traveling *mummers*."

Mary felt safe with her friends gathered close.

"Mary Bunyan, my son, Gifre, has something to say to you," said an unfamiliar man's voice. "First, please allow me to apologize for myself. Gifre learned his anger at my knee. I allowed political loyalties to color my life."

"Political loyalties?" asked Mary.

"I am a *royalist*. During the years of the *Protectorate*, I became embittered. My bitterness spilled over onto my son—I excuse him not one whit, understand, but the fault lies at my door as well." He cleared his throat. "I spoke out against your father and the *dissenters* many a time. My son took it personally and, understanding how much you mean to your father, Gifre lashed out at your father by hurting you."

Mary did not know what to say, so she remained quiet.

"I knew naught of Gifre's bullying, but this morning the story was all over Bedfordshire. I could not credit it—mine

own son! I walked to the place they said the attack happened."
His voice sounded sorrowful. "I found my rope still swinging
from the branch, then I saw the cloth with the shattered jug
and spoon. Gifre, what have you to say to Mary Bunyan?"

"Sorry." The voice was little more than a sullen growl
and Mary knew the sentiment was not heartfelt.

"Gifre spent all morning polishing your father's spoon."
He put the spoon in Mary's hand. "We used my son's egg
money to buy this jug to replace the broken one." He laid it
on the bed beside her.

Mary could tell it was a fine jug. It was glazed stoneware
in place of the biscuitware mug that had broken. It had a
pewter hinged top that would keep Papa's soup warm all the
way to the jail.

"Thank you, Gifre," Mary said.

Gifre grunted.

"And this leather pouch holds the jug and spoon, along
with a small table covering. The tanner, Winswode, worked
all morning to make this for you. Gifre gave him two chickens
in exchange." Gifre's father cleared his throat. "'Twill not
make up for the damage done by my son, but, by my oath,
Gifre will never hear a bitter word come from my mouth
again."

"Thank you, sir. And thank you, Gifre, for your generous
replacements."

Again Gifre only grunted.

"Good day to you then." The boy's father sounded embarrassed.

Mary could tell from the scuffling of Gifre's feet that her
tormentor did not share a change of heart with his father.

That was a problem she could do nothing about, but she smiled to realize that she could let God handle that problem.

As Elizabeth and the others saw the father and son out the door, Sofia pressed something into Mary's hand. "I think you will not refuse a gift from me, will you, friend?"

Mary knew it was Timoz's cross.

"That is to remind you of our faith, while I am on *O Longo Drom*."

"Thank you, Sofia." Mary reached out her arms and Sofia leaned into the embrace. "I will treasure it always. Every time I feel the nails of this cross, I will remember the great sacrifice. I will also remember that I no longer have to do all things alone. I have Jesus—*Yeshua*—and I have friends."

Mary heard Elizabeth cry out as the door opened. "What is it, Sofia?" Mary asked. "Can you see?" She could hear talking all at once and a booming voice. *Could it be?*

"Is that my wee Mary, looking like she tangled with Timoz's bear?"

"Papa!" Mary could not believe her ears. "Are you free?" She felt her father sit gently on the bed. She caught the faint scent of rosemary.

"No, I have not been freed. Not yet. My jailer accompanied me. He is having a glass of pear cider with Bets at this very moment." Papa laughed.

"'Tis so good to hear your voice in this cottage again, Papa. Elizabeth? Are you here?" Mary asked.

"Aye," said Elizabeth. "I am right beside him, drinking in the joy of his visit as well."

"Look what I have, Mary." He laid a bundle of tagged

laces across her hands. "Just in time to give to my good friend Timoz."

"They are fine laces, Neighbor Bunyan. We shall have no problem making a nice profit on these," said Timoz. "And here is the coin to pay for them, Mary."

"Not me, Timoz," laughed Mary. "From now on, Elizabeth will be managing the family finances."

"I must take *O Puri Daj* and Sofia to join the *kumpania*. Time has come to roll our wagons out." Timoz squeezed Mary's hand.

*I Puri Daj* lifted Mary's hand to her mouth and kissed the palm. Sofia kissed Mary on the cheek.

"In the spring, Mary," promised Sofia.

"Aye. I will wait for spring." Something seemed to tug from deep inside as her friend moved to leave—almost as though they were connected. Mary reached out to take Timoz's cross.

"Godspeed, my friends," said Papa as Mary heard the door close.

"What is this, Mary?" asked Papa.

Mary told Papa about her newfound faith. As she reached her fingers up to see Papa's face once again, she felt his tears. She knew he understood that she had finally left her heavy burden at the foot of the cross.

Papa kissed her forehead and went to spend some time alone with Elizabeth and to visit with Bets, Jake, and little Thomas. Mary loved listening to the sounds of happy voices in the cottage once again.

Papa would soon leave to return to Bedford *Gaol.* They did not know what the future would hold, but as she drifted off to sleep, Mary repeated a familiar verse—"I can do all things," but she would never again forget the second part, "through Christ which strengtheneth me."

# Epilogue

$\mathcal{M}$ary Bunyan was a real person. She was born in 1650 in Elstow, England, some 350 years ago. Her family—Papa, Elizabeth, Bets, Jake, and Thomas—were also real. Others—like Sofia, *O Puri Daj*, Timoz, and Gifre—are fictional. The *Rom* traveled the length and breadth of the British Isles during Mary's day, and a more complex *Legend of the Crucifixion Nails* is still told among *Roma*.

Mary went to be with her Lord in the spring of 1663.* She was sorely missed by her family and friends, but Mary Bunyan will never be remembered as a tragic figure. The picture that is indelibly etched in history is the ten-year-old blind daughter making the daily journey to the Bedford *Gaol*, carrying her father's supper.

---

*History doesn't record the cause of Mary's death, only that she became sick and died. Most likely her illness was bubonic or pneumonic plague. These were epidemic in England during this period. 1664–6 marked the years of the Great London Plague.

Mary's father, John Bunyan, lived in Bedford *Gaol* for the greater part of fourteen years, though he was occasionally allowed freedom to preach and visit his family when accompanied by his jailer. It was during his time in jail that he wrote his famous *Pilgrim's Progress,* which has sold more copies than any book in history except the Bible. Some of the ideas that you read about in *The Tinker's Daughter*—like the Slough of Despond and leaving our burden at the foot of the cross—come from *Pilgrim's Progress.*

John Bunyan's uncanny ability to paint a picture with words may have come from his deep relationship with Mary, who, in his own words, "lay nearer my heart than all I had besides." In addition to his writing and preaching, which has forever changed the world, John Bunyan made tagged laces "many hundred gross" by his own admission.

# Glossary

**Apothecary vials.** Small glass containers for medicine.

**Assizes.** English county court sessions.

**Baba.** The *Romani* word for grandmother.

**Baiting.** A mixture of dung and water that opens the pores of the leather to make the leather smooth in the process of tanning.

**Baiting dub.** The vat that holds the *baiting* mixture.

**Boria.** The *Romani* word for sisters-in-law.

**Casket.** A box.

**Chemise.** A one-piece undergarment like a slip.

**Chey.** The *Romani* word for girl.

**Curried.** Finished leather.

**Daft.** Insane or silly.

**Dissenter.** A person who did not agree with and follow the rules of the official Church of England.

**Dovecote.** A house built for doves.

**Firebell.** A clay bell-shaped cover with a handle at the top that was used to safely cover the remains of a fire and keep the ash smoldering.

**Furlong.** A distance that is 220 yards or 201 meters long.

**Gadje.** The *Romani* word for anyone who is not *Rom*.

**Gallows.** The structure from which criminals were hung as a form of capital punishment.

**Gaol.** Jail.

**Gristle.** Cartilage.

**Groat.** A coin worth four English pennies.

**Hippocras.** Spiced wine with honey.

**I Puri Daj; O Puri Daj.** The *Romani* terms for grandmother.

**Jongleur.** A traveling minstrel.

**Kumpania.** A group of families who travel together.

**Leading strings.** Strips of fabric sewn to the child's clothing at the shoulders that were used to help children learn to walk. Also used to control children's movements.

**Leeches.** Worms that suck blood.

**Lime. limes, limed.** A powdery white substance from limestone or shells used in the process of tanning leather.

**Lungo Drom; O Longo Drom.** The long road, or the journey that *Rom* people traveled.

**Mahrime.** Unclean.

**Marchpane.** Marzipan, a candy made of sweet almond paste.

**Maslin.** Dry bread that is half rye and half wheat.

**Mechanick.** A manual laborer.

**Minstrel.** A medieval entertainer who sang.

**Mummer.** A mime.

**Mutton.** Meat from a mature sheep.

**Nonconformist.** A person who did not agree with and follow the rules of the official Church of England.

**O Puro Dad.** The *Romani* term for grandfather.

**Oozing.** Powdered oak bark.

**Pallet.** A bed.

**Pantalets.** Long underpants worn by women.

**Peaky.** Sickly.

**Peat.** A moss that was dried and used as fuel for fires.

**Plat.** An area of land.

**Pommage.** Apple cider.

**Popinjay.** A very proud person who likes to show off.

**Protectorate.** The English government (1654–60) under Oliver Cromwell that allowed religious freedom.

**Pure.** Animal dung.

**Restoration.** In 1660 the *Protectorate* was defeated, monarchy was restored, and religious expression limited.

**Rom.** A nomadic people group. Also known as Gypsies.

**Romani.** The language spoken by *Rom*.

**Royalists.** Those who supported the monarchy.

**Shire.** A county in England.

**Stone.** Fourteen pounds.

**Suckets.** Sweetmeats.

**Swoon.** Faint.

**'Swounds.** A vulgar word that referred to the wounds of Jesus.

**Yeshua.** The *Romani* word for Jesus.

**Yeshua ben Miriam.** The *Romani* term for Jesus, Son of Mary.

**Zuhho.** The *Romani* word for pure or clean.

# Further Insights by Moody Press

## *COURAGE TO RUN*

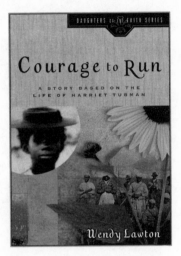

Born Arminta Ross, young Harriet Tubman (named after her mother when she was full-grown) was a faithful strong girl growing up in the late 1800's as a slave in the south. Her faith was at the center of everything she did and she was tested at every turn.

The story of her childhood is a record of courage and bravery. Even more, it's the story of God's faithfulness as he prepares her to eventually lead more than 300 people out of slavery through the Underground Railroad.

ISBN: 0-8024-4098-3, Paperback

Moody Press, a ministry of Moody Bible Institute,
is designed for education, evangelization, and edification.
If we may assist you in knowing more about Christ
and the Christian life, please write us without obligation:
Moody Press, c/o MLM, Chicago, Illinois 60610.